HIS SALVATION

SHINING ARMOR #3

CHARITY PARKERSON

--Warning: This book is intended for readers over the age of 18.

Copyright © 2018 Charity Parkerson
Editor: Hercules editing and Consultants
Photographer: Joshua Howard| Green Owl Photography
Cover model: Gus Caleb Smyrnios
ISBN: 978-1-946099-31-0
All rights reserved.

❀ Created with Vellum

INTRODUCTION

JAYDEN IS THE GUY EVERYONE WANTS.
UNTIL THEY HAVE HIM, THAT IS. NOW
HE'S DONE WITH LOVE.

For months, Jayden tried winning back his ex while being chased by Darrel. It seemed like the minute he gave in to Darrel and the man won his heart, Darrel was done. That seems to be Jayden's lot in life. Men want him until they have him. He's the thrill of the chase. Now he's done with men. With his broken heart held tight to his chest, Jayden intends to head to California and start over. Fate has other plans. One last day on the job is all that stands between Jayden and a new life. That, and the man holding him hostage at the bank.

Darrel has loved no one other than Jayden. It's not Jayden's fault Darrel is a screw-up. That's all on Darrel. He's never been good at holding a relationship together. That doesn't mean he intends to let Jayden get away. There's only one problem; he has to keep the man alive if he hopes to win him back. There's no lengths Darrel won't go to for Jayden. Even if it means Darrel has to walk away from Jayden, saving the man from him.

CHAPTER 1

"A FEMALE, APPROXIMATELY SIXTY-TWO-YEARS OLD, having symptoms of cardiac arrest."

Jayden listened to the details as he weaved through traffic while never letting up on his horn. "Citizen Union First Bank on Dower Street." Jayden turned left, trying to avoid the backup from cars leaving the nearby high school that had just released five minutes earlier. Teenagers always seemed to panic when they heard sirens. His mind raced as he drove. He had a patient, and he didn't know if he could get to her, since she was currently being held hostage. Jayden knew there was a real possibility he might have to stand on the sidelines while she died. He hated that. It was his job to help people. It wasn't in his nature to let anyone suffer.

She was someone's family—maybe a mother, sister, or grandmother. Someone would miss her if Jayden couldn't get to her. All he could do was go, and hope the man currently holding fifteen people hostage inside Citizen Union would let the woman go, so Jayden could get her to the hospital.

As he turned right onto Dower, Jayden ran into a wall of emergency vehicles. His gaze shied away from the nearby SWAT trucks. Darrel might be here. Jayden couldn't think about that. He had a job to do. Treating this like any other job, he leapt into the fray, gathering his gear and heading for the frontlines. Tiffany, his partner, was right at his side, helping to maneuver their gurney through the crowd. He made it as far as the first line of vehicles before being stopped by the negotiator on duty.

The balding man held up his hand. Jayden nodded his understanding.

"The paramedics are here. All you have to do is send her out, and I promise no one will harm you."

The man listened and nodded as if the guy could hear his head bobbing before speaking again. "If you let her die, that's manslaughter at the very least. Up until now, you haven't hurt anyone. Don't make things harder on yourself." The man's light blue gaze landed on Jayden. Chills raced up Jayden's spine. "We can do that, but you'll have to open the door."

Jayden's heart sank. He had a bad feeling he'd stepped in some shit. When the man's gaze never wavered from Jayden, the sensation intensified. After all, this was Jayden's luck. It was his last day on the job. In less than a week, he'd be living in San Diego, enjoying the beach life. That is, if he lived through today.

"She's unconscious. You'll have to go in after her."

Without a qualm, Jayden headed for the door after a quick rundown of instructions. None of them stuck. There was too much going on inside his head. If he died, no one would miss him. That probably wasn't true of the woman inside, waiting for his help. There was nothing to decide. He had a job to do. Jayden fought the urge to look right and left, searching for any sign of Darrel. If this was his last day on earth, he hoped Darrel was here, so Jayden wouldn't be completely alone. Maybe Darrel didn't really love him, but Jayden loved him. The heart was stupid like that.

PLEASE DON'T LET *it be Jayden.* The silent chant inside Darrel's head wouldn't stop. With the ninety-seven-degree heat suffocating him while he held his position in full SWAT gear, Darrel begged every entity who might be listening. It couldn't be Jayden. At exactly nine a.m., a man of unknown age and origin had walked inside Citizen Union First Bank and taken fifteen people hostage. That was a normal day for Darrel. Then, one of the hostages— a sixty-two-year-old female—had gone into cardiac arrest, changing the game. Still, Darrel had stayed calm. This was his job. That is, until their suspect had agreed to allow two paramedics inside to treat the woman. Jayden had been one. Ten minutes later, only one paramedic had been permitted to leave with the cardiac patient. Darrel couldn't deal. He could only see the back door. Waiting to hear if it was Jayden who'd been left behind was killing him.

Jayden Florakis was the greatest love of Darrel's life. Had been ever since the first time Darrel set eyes on the man. Most people might not believe in love at first sight. In truth, Darrel had always thought it was bullshit too. Then he'd met Jayden. The moment he'd set eyes on the man, every ridiculous cliché thing he'd ever heard came true. He swore violins played somewhere in the distance. Clouds parted, and the sun shone brighter. Jayden was of Greek descent and was every bit the Adonis —brown hair, beautiful green eyes, and perfect body. He had been smiling, showing the world's sexiest dimples. Jayden hadn't smiled much since. That was all on Darrel. As much as it had been love at first sight, Darrel had been unequipped for such a change in his life. He'd been so focused on winning Jayden, he hadn't considered what it would be like once he had him. Darrel had never considered how his own jealousy would drive him to do things he could never take back—unforgivable things. Now Jayden was in danger, and all Darrel had was regrets and things left unsaid.

"Jayden didn't come out."

Darrel's heart slammed against the wall of his chest as his partner Wyatt's voice came through his earpiece. Since Darrel covered the back door, he didn't have eyes on the exchange. He was at Wyatt's mercy. Darrel tried several times to respond. His mouth opened, but no sound emerged. He blinked, fighting the urge to storm the building. Only his training stopped him. He knew he'd be more likely to get Jayden killed by pulling something stupid, but he needed Jayden out of that building.

Finally, Darrel managed to make his voice work, but his words came out sounding pained, even to him. "Wyatt, don't let my man die."

"Sniper has eyes on him."

Darrel tried taking a calming breath. It didn't work. All he could think about was the last time they'd spoken.

Inside the county courthouse, standing at Bryce and Richie's back, watching them marry with Jayden at his side was rough. It felt real—like he could picture marrying Jayden. This could be their wedding. Before the ceremony, he'd tried talking to Jayden with no luck. The moment the formalities were at an end, Darrel was back, doing his damnedest to get Jayden to speak with him.

He cut the man off from the herd. "I miss you."

"I'm leaving."

A growl rose in Darrel's throat. "Fuck. Don't do that. Bryce is your best friend. He'll hate me more than he already does if you leave."

Jayden's gorgeous green gaze moved over Darrel's face, as if searching for something only he could see. "That's not what I meant. I've been offered a position in San Diego." Darrel took the news like a punch to the throat. He couldn't speak. "I'm putting in my two weeks' notice tonight."

"San Diego," Darrel repeated, because his brain wouldn't work, but his tongue did. "Huh." That was all Darrel had. Darrel couldn't decide if he loved Jayden enough to watch him leave and be happy, or if he would fight and make him happy here. Either way, Darrel felt ill-equipped. "That's only a five-hour drive. I could make that." Even he had no idea where the words came from, but they were true. He'd make the drive every damn weekend if Jayden would take him back.

A smile snapped to Jayden's face, lighting the man from the inside out. He shook his head. "You couldn't stay faithful to me with me living in the same house as you." Jayden's smile turned self-deprecating. "It's fine, Darrel. I'll be better there."

Darrel shook his head. "I don't think I've ever been this speechless while having so much to say."

"It's okay," Jayden said. His expression turned understanding, making Darrel want to break shit. Jayden shouldn't be the one trying to comfort him. Darrel didn't deserve consolation. "It's not your fault. Not really. It's me. It's always been this way for me. I'm like that toy everyone wants for Christmas. You know, the one you fight and beg for, but once you have it, you realize it's kind of boring, and you lose interest right away." Jayden swallowed as if the confession hurt his throat. "That's not on you."

Too many times to count, since that

conversation, Darrel had wondered why he didn't fight. Why didn't he try harder? He could have said any number of things to change Jayden's mind. At the time, he'd thought he would have another chance. A chance that wasn't encroaching on their friends' wedding. Now he realized that wasn't true. Jayden was inside that bank, and Darrel might not get to say any of the things he needed to say.

"Negotiations are breaking down. It looks like we'll be going in. Everyone into position."

Darrel prayed harder. Storming the building increased the risk of injury. It wasn't his job to make that call. Only the people in charge could know what happened to bring them to this point, but he knew going in meant the danger to the hostages was imminent. He couldn't let Jayden get hurt. His usual calm was nonexistent. Darrel's stomach cramped. His heart raced as he crouch-walked to the corner, ready to bolt inside on command. A countdown began in his ear. Darrel shifted onto the balls of his feet, ready to move. Before the count made it to five, a spate of gunfire erupted. Darrel made it three steps. An explosion threw him off his feet. He scrambled to recover. Nothing mattered any longer. No one would stop him from getting to Jayden. There was a tiny part of his brain that recognized he might be too late. Jayden might be dead. He had to know. He had to get to Jayden. If Jayden was okay, Darrel swore he'd make things right. He'd undo the damage he'd caused if was the last thing he ever did. If Jayden survived that blast, Darrel would fix everything.

CHAPTER 2

LIFE BECAME A BLUR, WHOOSHING BY WHILE NOT moving anywhere near quickly enough. The images in his head wouldn't abate. Jayden's body, covered in blood, would live in his mind forever. He wasn't family. No one would tell Darrel anything. With his SWAT gear still covering his body, Darrel sat in the waiting room of Sand Valley General Hospital not caring the least about his discomfort. His mind was firmly locked on Jayden. His knees bobbed. He'd chewed all his fingernails down past the quick an hour ago. Not knowing was making him insane. Bryce rushed through the door, his face set. As usual, even under the worst of circumstances, the man didn't have a single hair out of place and his suit was perfectly pressed. Darrel was good under pressure, but he'd never met anyone who held a candle to Bryce. Nothing ever seemed to get to him.

Darrel flew to his feet, intercepting Bryce. "They won't tell me anything."

With a nod, Bryce headed for the window. Darrel lingered behind him, biting his nonexistent nails. A few quiet words were exchanged, and Bryce waved for Darrel to follow him as the nurse buzzed them back to the depths of the ER. Darrel waited until they were through the door before bombarding Bryce with questions.

"How did you do that? I've been trying to get an update since we arrived. Why are they letting us back now? What did they say?"

Bryce glanced over. The light hit his face at just the right angle. Darrel realized Bryce was nowhere near as calm as he appeared. Every muscle in the man's face was tight. There was a slight panic to his light green eyes. "Jayden gave me power of attorney a few months back, since he has no one else. We still can't see him, but there's a different waiting room back here where they'll keep us posted."

"Why can't we see him? Is it that bad? Why did he give you power of attorney instead of his grandmother?" Darrel couldn't stop. Nervousness used his tongue as a weapon, keeping him sane.

Bryce set his hand on Darrel's shoulder. Immediately, some of the tension left him. This was what Bryce did. He was a psychologist who'd treated government employees—FBI, CIA, and DEA agents for years who'd seen things no one should. The man was in his element. "Jayden's in ICU. They won't let us see him until he's stable. Jayden had to put his grandmother in a nursing home last month. Dementia has fully taken hold of her, and he can't care for her any longer. All he has is me. Have a seat," he said, urging Darrel toward a pair of chairs in a quiet corner.

Darrel sat. He wanted to scream that Jayden had him too. Darrel had lost that privilege—thrown it away. He'd never felt more useless. The ways he'd failed Jayden kept adding up. "What did they say?"

Bryce didn't respond right away. He sat and focused on Darrel. The man's sympathetic gaze did nothing to comfort him. If anything, his fear ratcheted up. "Tell me what happened."

Darrel took a breath. He understood Bryce was trying to talk him away from the ledge by taking him back to the scene, walking him through like a professional. "There were fifteen hostages inside. Negotiations were taking a long time but were moving in the right direction. Then we received word that one of the hostages had gone into cardiac arrest. Paramedics were called." Darrel took another deep breath, finding calm in the retelling. "Jayden arrived with his usual partner, Tiffany. The suspect agreed to let paramedics inside, but once they were in, he wouldn't let them leave with their patient unless one of them agreed to take her place. Of course, you know Jayden." Darrel's eyes fell closed. He'd known the moment Jayden had gone in, he wouldn't come out. Jayden was a good person all the way to his bones. He cared about people. If he thought he could help, he would. His eyes reopened. He found Bryce watching him. After another deep breath, Darrel continued. "From what I understand, the suspect was getting antsy. Things he requested were taking too long to come to fruition. He knew he was being strung along. Negotiations were breaking down. We were ordered to go in. Before we made it, an armed security guard inside the building finally worked up some nerve and shot the guy. Unfortunately, the guy was wired to blow, and we didn't know it." Every breath came harder than the last until Darrel thought he might have to put his head between his knees to stave off a panic attack.

Darrel sucked air.

Bryce rubbed his back. "We should know something soon."

"Is he dating someone? We should call them if he is. They should be here." Darrel just wanted to take care of Jayden, even if that meant calling some random guy who'd taken his place.

"There's just us," Bryce said with a shake of his head. "His grandmother doesn't even remember him any longer. Richie is holding down the fort, cancelling all my appointments for the day. Benny says Wyatt is still on the scene. They'll come together once Wyatt gets home, but it could be a while."

A blond man wearing green scrubs and a white coat rounded the corner. "Dr. Tuthill," the man said, dragging Bryce's attention his way.

Bryce came to his feet. "I'm Dr. Tuthill."

The man held out his hand. "Dr. Vincent. Nice to meet you," he said, shaking Bryce's hand. "I'm in charge of Jayden's care."

Bryce nodded. "How is he?"

The way the man's chest expanded before he spoke didn't give Darrel much hope. Neither did the man's dark tone. "He's stable, for now. Luckily, he

Follow this hall to the end and make a left. His room is the last one on the right."

Darrel didn't need to be told twice. He was already heading Jayden's way before the man finished giving directions. The moment he crossed the threshold of the trauma room, Darrel's steps slowed. The top half of Jayden's head was covered in thick bandages. Machines lit and flashed, keeping time with his heartbeat and oxygen level. Bryce touched his shoulder, and Darrel moved closer. He couldn't bring himself to sit. His gaze moved over Jayden, inspecting every inch he could see. The man's lip was cut open. A long gash marred his chin and neck. Jesus. If the cut had been deeper, the glass might have taken out an artery. Darrel swallowed. His eyes burned. He swallowed again.

"Dear God."

Bryce kept rubbing his back. The motion did nothing to warm his chilled skin. "He'll live. That's all that matters."

Darrel wanted to scream. That wasn't all that mattered. Jayden didn't deserve this. Darrel wanted to kiss him and touch him everywhere, ensuring he was whole, but he'd lost that right. He had no one to blame but himself. Everything burned—like fire ants tore at his skin. He needed Jayden to wake up and hit him—the way he should've done months ago.

"This is a fucking nightmare." Darrel meant everything. Not just today. Every day he'd woken up since losing Jayden was a horrible dream he couldn't shake. No one understood because he was the one in the wrong. There was no pity for him. No one knew how much he tormented himself. Now, this. It should've been him.

"Okay, sit down," Bryce said, urging him toward the chair beside the bed. "Here's what you're going to do. You need to sit right here, as close to Jayden as possible, and soak him in. Trust me, no one understands like I do."

That was true. Bryce's husband Richie had been held captive for two months and came home half-alive. If anyone understood his distress, it was Bryce.

Darrel sat. Bryce massaged his shoulders. "I'll run home, grab Richie, and come back in a few hours. For now, you can stare at him until your nerves settle—without witnesses. I know having people watching you, waiting for your breakdown, is half the problem." He bent and kissed Darrel's cheek. "Jayden won't leave us. You can do this. He needs you to be strong now."

With Bryce's reassurances still hanging in the air, even after he left, Darrel managed a modicum of calm. He stared at the monitor that showed Jayden's heartbeat. The sight brought him comfort. As long as Jayden lived, Darrel could survive anything. He would endure anything. A gasp sounded from the bed, sending a jolt through Darrel. He had no idea how long he'd sat in the same spot, waiting, and watching Jayden breathe. It could've been hours or minutes. The heart monitor went nuts as Jayden tried scrambling from the bed while still attached to machines and an IV. Darrel flew to his feet and urged Jayden back down.

"Shhh. It's okay. Calm down. You're in the hospital."

Jayden sucked in several audible breaths. "Why can't I see?"

"You have retina burns from the explosion. Do you remember anything?"

The alarm on the heart monitor stopped blaring, but Jayden's heart rate didn't slow by much. He took several more labored breaths. "Not really, no. Who are you?"

The question gave Darrel pause. He hadn't expected Jayden to not know him. "It's Darrel."

"Darrel? What's wrong with your voice?"

Despite everything, a smile tugged at Darrel's lips. It was just like Jayden to be in the hospital and worry over someone else. "Don't worry about that right now. What's the last thing you remember?"

Jayden settled down. His heart rate finally dropped. "I got a call for a cardiac arrest at a bank."

Darrel nodded, forgetting for a moment Jayden couldn't see him. "There was a hostage situation at the bank. One of the hostages went into cardiac arrest. You went in."

Jayden nodded. "He wouldn't let us leave unless one of us agreed to take her place."

"You stayed," Darrel said, keeping the story moving forward.

"He made me get on the floor. Before I was completely down, he rushed across the room, screaming something at someone I couldn't see. That's all I know."

Darrel sat on the bed, holding Jayden's hand. He half expected Jayden to pull away any minute. Instead, Jayden held tight—like Darrel was a lifeline. "There was a guard no one had realized was armed. He pulled his gun. The suspect was wired. There was an explosion."

Jayden's heart raced up again. "What?"

Darrel held tighter to Jayden's hand. "Since you were across the room and by a window, you were thrown clear. You've got some cuts and bruises. As well as some flash burns on your retinas. Your eardrums burst, but I see you can still hear. They should heal fine." Darrel smiled as he said the words. He was so damn glad Jayden could still hear. It was something, at least.

Jayden's chest rose as he took a deep breath. "There's a slight ringing in my ears, but that's all." He took another breath. Darrel knew he was trying to stay calm. "What are they saying about my eyes?"

"You need time," Darrel said, trying to sound like it wasn't a big deal. He needed to be calm and upbeat for Jayden. "They have to keep them covered, so they can rest and heal."

Jayden stayed quiet for so long Darrel wanted to scream. He didn't know how to fix a reaction Jayden wasn't having. Jayden licked his lips. "What's wrong with your voice?"

Unexpectedly, Darrel's eyes burned. Darrel swallowed—hard, trying to fight back the tears. He loved this man. Nothing bad was supposed to happen to Jayden. It wasn't fair for such a good person to be in this position. Darrel cleared his throat. It hurt. "My team was there, getting ready to go in, when the bomb exploded."

Jayden's grip tightened on Darrel's hand. "Are you okay? What about Wyatt?"

The burning sensation behind Darrel's eyes increased. He took another breath. "We're all fine. The smoke burned my throat," Darrel lied, because he didn't have the strength to confess to screaming himself hoarse, searching for Jayden.

"Why are you sitting here with me? You should be getting checked out." Jayden sounded tired—like he was fighting the pain medication to stay awake.

He rubbed Jayden's arm. "I'm fine. Don't worry over me."

Jayden didn't respond right away. Darrel checked his vitals. They were steady. "What about the woman?"

Darrel blinked. Jayden sounded half asleep, making him wonder if Jayden was talking out of his head. "What woman?" Darrel whispered, in case Jayden was more asleep than awake.

"My cardiac patient."

"I'll check on her," Darrel promised, hoping Jayden would rest. So far, Jayden hadn't asked him to leave. He wasn't sure that would hold forever. "Bryce will be back soon with Richie. I'm sure he'll grab anything you need from your place. I'll check on your grandmother. Do you need me to do anything else?"

"Stay," Jayden said, sounding weak.

Darrel swallowed past the lump in his throat. "I'm not going anywhere." He didn't reclaim his seat until he was certain Jayden slept. Even then, he couldn't take his eyes off Jayden. Darrel's teeth chattered. He clenched his jaw against the sensation. The idea of Jayden not existing in the world somewhere even if they weren't together—it was too much. There was still a part of him that wanted to fight. He loved Jayden. Always would. Jayden taking him back would be like having his dreams come true. But the day's events shone light on the truth, Jayden deserved happiness. To truly live. He wouldn't find those things with Darrel. Darrel had already proven he wasn't worthy. He would stay because he'd told Jayden he would. But he wouldn't bother the man again after this. Once Jayden was better, Darrel would walk away, and let the man be. The way he should've done a long time ago.

JAYDEN RACED TO GET HOME. Darrel was waiting. He'd told the man to call if he had any complications from his shoulder surgery. That was the only reason Darrel would seek him out. Jayden couldn't get there fast enough. As he tore into the driveway, he spotted Wyatt on the porch, relaxing in a lawn chair.

Jayden took a calming breath before climbing from his car. He needed to keep a cool head. His mouth didn't let him make it to the porch. "Are you okay? It's hard to tell tone from a text. Is your arm bothering you?"

Darrel glanced down at the sling holding his arm in place. "No. Sorry, I didn't mean to worry you."

A sigh rose in Jayden's throat. He swallowed it down before it escaped. His steps slowed. "That's okay. As long as you're all right."

"I'm not all right," Darrel said with a shake of his head, kicking Jayden's heart rate up again. "Can we talk inside?"

Jayden pulled out his keys and unlocked his door. He kept his gaze fixed on his hands while all the possibilities raced through his mind. Darrel wanted to talk. Nothing good could come of that. Cool air slapped him in the face as the door swung open. His gaze skirted the room, taking in the mess he'd left. There was a towel on the couch, socks on the floor, and a dirty glass on the table. He hadn't expected company, and since he'd stayed with Bryce the night before, he hadn't had time to clean.

"Sorry about the mess."

A snort sounded behind him. "Your place is always clean, especially compared to mine."

Jayden couldn't let himself think about Darrel's house. That was where they'd made love for the first time. Where they'd talked about living for good when Darrel claimed he wanted to marry Jayden. The place where he'd caught Darrel with someone else. Jayden rubbed his chest. The pain never lessened.

He tossed his keys on the table by the door. "What do you need to talk about?"

Darrel closed the door behind him before focusing on Jayden. "I know I don't deserve it, but I'm hoping you'll give me another chance."

It was a shot to the chest. Jayden's heartbeat sounded loud inside his ears. He couldn't breathe. "I'm sorry. What?"

"I want you back." He looked so goddamn confident— like he'd thought things through and had no doubts.

Jayden had doubts. He had misgivings for days. Why should Darrel question anything? Jayden had been damn good to him, given him everything. Darrel should've come crawling back ages ago. Jayden was the one who'd gotten fucked. He took a breath. Even to him, it sounded ragged. "What?" Fuck. He had no idea why nothing else would budge from his lips. Jayden had shit to say. He had lots and lots of things to say.

"I fucked up. We were moving fast, and—"

"We were moving fast because you were moving us," Jayden spat, finding his voice.

Darrel held up his hand. "I know. Just listen. Before you came along, I didn't know it was possible to love someone like I love you."

Not loved, but love—like present tense. Jayden heard it. He wanted to punch the man in the dick. Darrel wasn't through.

"You scared the fuck out of me because I'd never been so thoroughly owned by anyone. I freaked, but things weren't what they se—"

"Get the fuck out." The words flew from Jayden with a hate-filled fervor that shocked even him.

Darrel didn't budge.

"I'm serious," Jayden said, pointing toward the door. "You don't get to come here after you've fucked someone else and say this shit to me. Get out."

"I love you," Darrel said. His sincerity dampened some of Jayden's fury, and Jayden hated him for it. "I'm in love with you, Jayden. For real, I don't want anyone else ever again. You're it for me."

A tired-sounding sigh escaped Jayden. "Look, I

appreciate you trying to make things right. Maybe if things were different or if we'd met before—"

"I swear by all that's holy, if you say we were only a case of bad timing, I'll break the fucking clock in here just to prove you wrong," Darrel said, cutting him off and closing the distance between them. "What are you so scared of?"

Jayden growled and paced away before moving back to stand toe to toe with Darrel. "Do you mean besides having you break me again?"

"You know I'd cut out my heart before hurting you again, so yeah."

Jayden gave him a sharp nod, hearing the truth in his words. The least he could do was give Darrel the same honesty. "Fine. I'm terrified you'll tear down my walls and realize there's nothing behind them you really want. Then what? I don't have anyone to save me when you—once again—realize I'm not enough. Love takes hostages, Darrel, and I'm always the victim. I'm tired. I don't want to play anymore."

Jayden came awake with a start, gasping for air. He had no idea why the memory of Darrel always haunted his dreams, but the man was there waiting for him more often than not. Someone squeezed his hand.

"Darrel?"

"No, baby," Bryce said. "I made him go home.

He was still wearing his gear and starting to get ripe. Plus, he looked like hell. I told him he could come back after he'd showered, eaten, and taken a nap."

Jayden took a breath. Even to him it sounded ragged. "Thanks. I don't want anyone running themselves down for me."

Bryce rubbed his arm. "Of course. That's who you are. Always worrying about everyone else more than yourself. How are you feeling?"

Because it was Bryce, Jayden's mouth ran with the truth. "Scared shitless, honestly. Otherwise, I'm not in pain or anything."

"I'll go find you something decent to eat. The tray they left looks awful."

At the sound of Richie's voice, Jayden swallowed back a groan. He hadn't known Bryce's husband was there. He hated looking weak. It was one thing for Bryce to witness him at his lowest. He didn't care for anyone else to see him this way.

"Thanks, Richie. Sorry. I didn't know you were here."

"No worries. Hospitals suck. I'll make sure you don't suffer the food, if nothing else." If Richie knew about anything, it was long hospital stays. The man had spent several weeks in the hospital after two months in captivity when an undercover investigation he'd been working went wrong. Since then, Richie had quit his job at the DEA. The man spent every waking moment with Bryce. Jayden should've known he'd be there.

"Scoot your skinny ass over," Bryce said, pulling Jayden's focus back his way. "I want to hold you. You scared the shit out of me. Oh my god. I don't know what I'd do if anything happened to you."

Jayden didn't hesitate making room for Bryce. He needed someone to hold him. As Bryce settled in beside him and wrapped his arms around him, Jayden felt an overwhelming need to make light of the situation. It was the only thing that stopped the shaking inside. "Careful. You don't want your husband getting jealous."

"Don't worry over me," Richie said, proving he hadn't left yet. "I already know he gives away half my hugs and kisses to you." As he made the claim, Richie leaned over and kissed Jayden's cheek before whispering. "It's okay, though. I get all his kinks." With a laugh that got farther away, Richie obviously headed for the door. "I'll let the two of you cuddle for a while in peace while I hunt and gather."

"Thank you." Jayden waited for a minute before adding, "Is he gone?"

Bryce snuggled closer. "Yep."

"He's being nice to me. Now I feel guilty for all the times I was a dick to him." To be fair, Richie had broken Bryce's heart once. The man was lucky Jayden hadn't sliced his brake lines.

"Nah. Richie has thick skin. Plus, he blames himself for stealing all our mutual friends when he left me. It's all good now. Everything in the past is water under the bridge. Now stop worrying about everyone else. What do you need?"

"To not go blind," Jayden said without missing a beat. He knew he could be real with Bryce in a way he couldn't with anyone else. "I don't have anybody. If they take these bandages off, and I can't see, what will I do? I won't be able to work. It's not like I have parents who'll take me in." Jayden's insides shook as he made the claim. Each time he woke up, reality settled in a little further.

Bryce's lips touched the shell of Jayden's ear and didn't budge. Warmth filled Jayden's chest. He loved Bryce. It wasn't a romantic love, but just as important. Maybe more so. "Don't think about any of that. You have me."

Jayden couldn't let it go. "I'm not your responsibility. You have a husband and a new business. It's not in me to become your burden."

He jumped as Bryce swatted his thigh. It didn't hurt, but the move surprised him. "Fuck all that noise. What if the shoe was on the other foot? Don't bother answering because I know you wouldn't leave me. I'm not leaving you. You're not a burden. I can more than afford to take care of you if you need me, and I will. Not to mention, Richie is wrong. I don't give you half his hugs and kisses. I take all yours." Bryce's soft laugh brushed Jayden's ear. "Everything that happens to you happens to me too. Don't ever forget that."

Jayden tried letting it go. He didn't want Bryce to have to take care of him. The thought made him feel sick, but Bryce was right. If the shoe was on the other foot, he'd take care of Bryce in a heartbeat and never feel like he was a burden. He had to shove his pride aside. No matter how much it stung. Exhaustion had him in its grip, especially with Bryce holding him. "I'm sorry."

"For what?" Bryce asked, sounding every bit as tired as Jayden felt.

"I'm having a hard time staying awake." Even to his ears, Jayden sounded half asleep already.

Bryce rubbed his chest and arms. "Don't worry over me. I didn't sleep at all last night, worrying over you. You don't have to entertain me. I'm having a hard time staying awake too."

Jayden turned his head and kissed Bryce. He smiled as he realized he caught him on the eyebrow. "Go to sleep." Fatigue tugged at his brain, pulling him into its haze before he had time for Bryce's response.

CHAPTER 3

DAYS RAN TOGETHER, PASSING WITH NO INPUT FROM Jayden. He felt a little stronger each time he awoke. The guys took turns sitting with him during the day, so he was never alone, but Bryce stayed with him each night. The nurses had given up trying to force Bryce from his bed. Once they realized his blood pressure was much lower when Bryce slept beside him, they'd all agreed Bryce was like Jayden's comfort pet. That was all it had taken for everyone to make Bryce as comfortable as possible too. He'd moved rooms twice, since he'd been there so long. Jayden was damn tired of being there.

Darrel sat with him while Bryce worked. Jayden expected to resent his presence. Instead, he was beyond grateful not to be alone. They'd given him more pain medicine a few minutes earlier.

Darrel wasn't saying a word, as if he knew Jayden wouldn't be awake much longer. Unfortunately, the silence was unnerving. Jayden didn't know how to break it. He opened his mouth, hoping something halfway intelligent would fall out. Before he could find anything, a knock sounded on the door a half second before Dr. Vincent announced himself.

"Hey, Jayden. It's Dr. Vincent. How are you feeling tonight?"

"I'm okay."

"I'll run to the cafeteria and grab a snack while you get looked over," Darrel said, his voice moving away from the bed.

Jayden flashed a smile, even though he wasn't sure if Darrel looked his way. "Okay."

The scraping sound of the railing of his bed lowering caused Jayden to jump. He hadn't realized anyone stood so close. "Is it okay if I sit so I can check your bandages?"

Jayden swallowed. His heart still raced from being snuck up on. "Sure."

His bed shifted. Dr. Vincent's heat pressed against Jayden's thigh as he leaned across him. Expensive-smelling cologne wafted over him. Jayden dipped his chin, trying to help Dr. Vincent reach him. The doctor tugged at the outer layer of bandages. "Are you in any pain?"

"Not really. They gave me something a few minutes ago. By my calculations, I'll be out in half an hour."

Dr. Vincent chuckled. "You're a lightweight."

A smile tugged at Jayden's lips. "I guess so. I've never been much of a drinker and haven't had many reasons to take pain meds. They hit me hard."

Silence filled the air while the doctor worked. When the man finally spoke, his words came out haltingly, as if he questioned if he should speak. "By the way, what you did—taking that woman's place so she could get help—that was very brave. You saved her life."

"Some would say it was stupidity," Jayden admitted with a laugh. "But I like helping people."

"That's a sentiment I can understand. You could've died, so I still say you were brave."

Jayden shrugged. "Honestly, I don't really have anything other than my job. I kept thinking about how much everyone else had to live for. It seemed I had the least to lose."

The doctor pulled at his bandages. "I think this is the first time I've been in here that your room wasn't packed full of your friends. Seems like you have a lot more than your job to me."

Having his eyes covered gave Jayden the freedom to speak honestly. If he couldn't see Dr. Vincent's judgment, it didn't happen. "My friends are great. I don't deny that, but they all have lives of their own. When this passes, they'll go back to them. I'll go back to being alone. I don't have any family," he explained, in case the doctor thought he was being maudlin. "My parents overdosed on heroin in a grocery store parking lot with me in the backseat when I was seven. My grandma raised me, but now she's in a nursing home with dementia. It's just me now."

Dr. Vincent was no longer touching him, but he hadn't moved away. Jayden could still feel the heat radiating from the man's thigh so close to his leg. "Did you become a paramedic because of the thing with your parents?"

Jayden nodded. The man was nice to talk to. "What made you want to be a doctor?"

A low chuckle filled the room. Goosebumps rose on Jayden's skin. No matter what the man looked like or how old he was, the doctor had a sexy laugh, Jayden couldn't unlearn that detail or stop wanting to know more. "Nothing quite so altruistic as your motives. My parents are doctors. Mom is a gynecologist. My dad is a heart surgeon. There was never much chance I'd do anything else."

Jayden couldn't stop smiling. He liked listening to Dr. Vincent talk. "Do you have any siblings?"

"A sister, River. She's an ophthalmologist."

The pride in the doctor's tone made Jayden twice as lonely. "Sounds like a nice family."

"They are, but hey," he said, his voice brightening. "I don't know a single person who'd shove their way in to my hospital bed and refuse to leave. You may not have family, but you have people who are passionate about your wellbeing. That says a lot about you."

A soft knock landed on the door, and the doctor moved away. His weight disappeared from the bed.

"Your friend is back from the cafeteria," the doctor said. "Everything is coming along fine. I'll be back in the morning. Do you have any questions or concerns?"

"How much longer do you think I'll be here?"

"Hmmm," Dr. Vincent hummed, as if thinking things over. "I think it's too soon to tell. You're not really in a position to care for yourself yet, and the pain meds are probably giving you an unreal sense of wellness. Once we cut that down, you'll feel these burns. Plus, the location of your injuries puts you at a higher risk for complications due to infection. We're still in a wait and see place right now."

Jayden nodded. "Okay. I'll see you in the morning. Well, not see, but you know."

"Is it okay if he has this?" Darrel asked, making Jayden wonder what "this" was.

"Sure. There are no diet restrictions other than whatever he does to stay so ridiculously in shape."

"It's youth," Darrel said. "He should eat this before time kicks him in the ass."

Both men laughed while Jayden blushed. He felt out of the loop on everything without his eyesight. "Have a good night, guys," Dr. Vincent said. The sound of the door closing followed his words.

The legs of the chair scraped the floor, moving closer to the bed. "I'll put the railing back up after I feed you this. We can't have you rolling out after the drugs kick in."

Jayden was kind of hungry. "What am I eating?"

"It's a surprise." The happiness in Darrel's voice had Jayden willing to agree to anything.

"You're enjoying this a bit too much."

"Maybe just a little, but you know you can trust me." The silence after Darrel's claim was swift and thick. Jayden couldn't think of a response. Darrel didn't let him dwell. "Open up."

Jayden did as told. Ice cold cream filled his mouth. Jayden didn't even have to consider it. He knew immediately what Darrel had given him. He swallowed and smiled. "Cookies and Cream ice cream."

"Yep. As soon as I saw it, I knew it had to be yours. How could I pass up getting you your favorite ice cream?"

"Thank you." Jayden hoped Darrel heard the sincerity in his voice and understood he meant for more than the ice cream.

"Eat," Darrel said, giving Jayden another bite. He waited until Jayden's mouth was full to respond. "You know I'd do anything for you. Our failed relationship aside, I love you. It would kill me if anything happened to you." Darrel kept shoveling ice cream in Jayden's mouth, keeping him from saying anything.

An unexpected pain sliced through his head and Jayden turned his face away. A cold spoon hit his cheek. Laughter bubbled in his throat despite the pain. "Am I covered in ice cream now?"

"I've got you," Darrel said, his voice moving closer. Warm lips touched his cheek. Jayden's breath caught in his throat. He went still, not daring to move. Darrel's tongue swiped his cheek before the man's mouth moved to the corner of Jayden's, lightly brushing. Jayden turned toward Darrel's touch. Their lips met.

Darrel moved away.

Jayden fought to breathe. His heart raced. He was damn glad they were no longer monitoring his heart rate. "You'll have to finish the ice cream. The pain meds are kicking my ass."

Darrel cleared his throat. "Do you want me to lean your bed back, so you can sleep?"

Jayden swallowed and nodded. He didn't trust his voice any longer. The scraping of the railing rent the air and his bed reclined. Jayden rolled to his side, facing Darrel. He waited until he was settled, and he no longer feared his voice cracking before speaking. "Darrel."

"Yeah."

"Our failed relationship aside, I love you too." As the claim left his lips, Jayden felt the loss of his sight harder than ever. In that moment, he would've given anything to see Darrel's face. He swallowed past the pain. "To this day, I still don't know why I failed so thoroughly at keeping you." The moment the words were out there, hanging between them,

Jayden wished like hell he could take them back. No good could come of exposing his heart. "Never mind. I'm just overly tired." Even to Jayden's ears, he heard the slur in his voice. Sometimes, when he was at his weakest—like now—Jayden found himself hoping for the unthinkable. There was a part of Jayden that wished he wouldn't wake up. He was exhausted. Jayden had never considered himself weak. Lately, he wasn't sure any longer. Tonight, he was a rickety soul built on a rotten foundation. Jayden had nothing left. Thankfully, everything fell away, stealing him from reality.

It was one o'clock in the morning. Jayden had just gotten off work. He was tired and hungry. More than anything, Jayden wanted to shower, eat something, and fall into bed with Darrel. A whole week of staycation was ahead of them. Jayden had no plans beyond keeping Darrel in bed as much as possible, cuddling and whatever else came up. It seemed Darrel had other plans.

Jayden didn't even get to take off his shoes before Darrel shuffled him back out the door. "What are you doing? I need a shower."

"No whining," Darrel fussed as he opened the passenger side of his truck and urged Jayden inside.

"But I'm hungry," Jayden said, purposely taking on a wheedling tone.

"There's food next to you."

Jayden looked down. Sure enough, sandwiches, chips, and drinks were waiting for him. He settled in. Whatever Darrel planned, Jayden would survive as long as there was food. He waited until they were on the interstate and he'd polished off a sandwich before questioning Darrel again.

"Where are we headed?"

Darrel kept his gaze locked on the road. "It's a surprise."

Jayden didn't let up. "How long will it take us to get there?"

"Eat and then get some sleep. I'll wake you up when we're there."

Jayden unwrapped a second sandwich. "Are you taking me to the dentist?"

A surprised-sounding bark of laughter escaped Darrel. "What?"

"You know," Jayden said around a bite. "They have those video clips online where parents tell their kids they're going to an amusement park, letting them get all excited, and then they go to the dentist."

Darrel shook his head. A sexy chuckle filled the truck. "Go to sleep."

After an hour of reading every passing road sign, trying to guess at their destination, Jayden finally drifted off. The smell of the ocean and the sound of waves crashing pulled him from his dreams.

This time, Jayden knew exactly where he was when the darkness met him. "Darrel."

"Yeah." The man sounded far away for some reason.

"I keep expecting to wake up to the smell of the ocean and the sound of waves crashing."

"If I could, I'd give that to you again."

Jayden fought against the meds. He didn't want to sleep. All the painful memories wouldn't abate, but even to him, his voice slurred with exhaustion when he spoke. "I'd rather you take the memories away, then it wouldn't hurt so much."

———

DARREL SWALLOWED SEVERAL TIMES. It sounded overly loud in the quiet room. He held the melted ice cream between his hands. His gaze never wavered from Jayden's face. He knew the man was asleep. Darrel had watched him sleep enough times to know the exact moment Jayden slipped away. Jayden's words haunted him. *I'd rather you take the memories away, then it wouldn't hurt so much.* Fuck. Jayden might as well have carved Darrel's heart out with a rusty spoon. His eyes burned, and his throat felt like he'd swallowed razor blades. He was a plague upon Jayden's life. As he'd fed Jayden ice cream, Darrel had craved Jayden's lips closing around something else every bit as hard as that spoon. One moment, he'd been watching Jayden lick his lips. The next, Darrel licked ice cream from the man's face. His lips had traveled to Jayden's mouth. He'd been incapable of stopping. Jayden could've died, and Darrel needed to taste him again. Then Jayden had opened his mouth and completely wrecked Darrel with that one claim. *To this day, I still don't know why I failed so thoroughly at keeping you.* As if he'd been at fault for Darrel's shortcomings.

Darrel couldn't fucking breathe. Hyperventilating looked like a real possibility. Each and every day, Darrel felt like he lost Jayden all over again. It was the slowest and most painful death. One he deserved. A warm hand landed on his shoulder, making Darrel jump. His gaze shot upward and landed on Bryce. The man looked blurry for some reason.

Bryce went down on his haunches. His face didn't clear. "Are you okay?" Bryce whispered.

Darrel couldn't answer. Replying required oxygen and Darrel was certain he'd never have that again.

Bryce grabbed the ice cream and set it aside before shoving Darrel's head down between his knees. "Breathe."

Darrel sucked air. The loud wheeze surprised even him. In a detached way, Darrel recognized everything was finally catching up with him. Realizing the facts didn't make them disappear. If anything, the dawning truth made everything seem realer than ever. He'd fucking lost Jayden. The man was gone. Darrel would never hold him again. He'd broken Jayden's heart—like he meant nothing. Darrel had violently destroyed the only person who meant a single fucking thing to him. He could never take it back.

"Come on," Bryce said, pulling Darrel to his feet and urging him toward the door.

When they hit the hallway, Darrel sucked more ragged breaths. Tears streamed down his cheeks, and he gave zero fucks what anyone thought about it. He deserved to hurt and to have everyone see him at his lowest. In fact, people should point and laugh, so he could face a drop of the humiliation Jayden had suffered for him.

"You need a break," Bryce said, rubbing his arms, as if trying to bring him back to reality. "I'm calling Richie to come get you."

Darrel shook his head. "You've spent too much time here. I'll stay. I'm fine."

Bryce snorted. "No. You're not. I planned to stay the night anyhow. You can keep Richie company for me. It's time for you to talk to someone and I know you won't talk to me."

"I don't need a shrink," Darrel argued, even though he wasn't sure that was true.

"That's not what I meant," Bryce said, dialing the phone. "You need a friend. Go out. Get drunk. Bare your soul, or don't. Just let go of this for one night. I'll call you if anything changes. Otherwise, I'll see you in the morning."

Darrel listened absently as Bryce called for Richie's help. Maybe the man was right. He needed to say the words in his head to someone he couldn't destroy. Richie would listen. Then, maybe the man would shoot him and put him out of Jayden's misery, because Darrel very much feared that was the only way he'd ever leave Jayden alone.

CHAPTER 4

DARREL NEVER WENT OUT ANYMORE. HE DIDN'T remember Jaks Tap being quite so filled with people half his age. The way Richie eyed their surroundings made Darrel wonder if he felt the same. Richie's blond hair was starting to gray at the temples and there were a few fine lines at the corners of his eyes. Even if the man didn't have those tell-tale signs, his deep scars made him look more rugged and worn than anyone else in the joint.

"Damn. I feel like I'm fucking Methuselah," Richie said, echoing Darrel's thoughts and making him laugh. Richie's gaze shot his way. "Wow. I don't think I've heard that sound in a while."

Confusion washed over him. "What?"

"Your laughter," Richie explained. "All you do is scowl and growl these days."

Darrel did a shot and chased it with his beer. "I'm old," he said, wincing through the burn. "Isn't that how crotchety old men are supposed to act?"

Before Richie could respond, a young blond guy with too much hair gel, wearing expensive cologne, appeared at Darrel's side. "Would you like to dance?"

Darrel's gaze moved between the kid and Richie. Richie's eyes danced with barely suppressed laughter. Darrel was filled with rage. He wasn't with Richie in a romantic sense, but they were sitting together. For all this guy knew, Richie was his date. "I'm taken," Darrel said, sounding gruffer than intended. The guy's overly bright smile fell, making Darrel feel like shit. He knew it took a lot courage to approach a stranger. "Thanks for asking, though," he added. "I'm flattered."

The guy's smile returned, and he nodded before disappearing as quickly as he'd appeared. When Darrel met Richie's stare again, the man eyed him while wearing an unreadable expression.

"What?"

Richie shook his head. "You."

Darrel looked down at himself before meeting Richie's gaze again. "What about me?"

"Why did you tell that guy you were taken? I don't care if you go dance. In fact, it might help your mood to let loose a little."

"I am taken," Darrel said, holding Richie's gaze, ensuring the man understood the truth. "I belong to Jayden until he tells me otherwise. You of all people should get that. Plus, that poor kid doesn't deserve to have me trample all over his life. Since my heart belongs to Jayden, that's all that would come of me getting to know him."

The more Darrel spoke, the darker Richie's expression turned. "I don't get it. Why did you cheat on Jayden if you plan to be faithful to him now?"

Irritation had Darrel snapping back, "Did you date anyone when Bryce and you split?"

"Of course not," Richie said as if it was understood, and it was. Darrel had known when he asked that Richie would never touch another man. Bryce was his whole world.

Darrel didn't miss his chance to be childish. "Then why did you leave the man if you planned to be faithful to him?"

Richie opened his mouth and floored Darrel,

making sure he felt as horrible as possible for being petty. "Because I planned to kill myself and I didn't want him to have to clean up the mess. He'd already spent six months trying to fix me when I was unfixable."

That shocked Darrel speechless. He'd known Richie had come home fucked up after the two months he spent in captivity with a drug lord. Until now, he hadn't realized how he'd failed at being Richie's friend every bit as much as he'd failed at being Jayden's man. "You should've said something."

Richie's mouth lifted in one corner. "You've had your own problems. Besides," he said, his tone turning light. "My husband is a psychologist. If I can't talk to him, everyone else is definitely a no go. It's okay. I didn't do it, and I found my way back. Everything worked out for the best."

"I only kissed that guy," Darrel said, admitting the truth about that day for the first time. "Well, he also had his hand down my pants, and I suppose it might've gone farther if Jayden hadn't come home. But I doubt it. I was already questioning my sanity and reasoning before Jayden got there."

There was no judgment in Richie's expression, but the pressure in Darrel's chest didn't ease. Richie didn't let him off the hook. "I had my own problems, so I wasn't a very good friend at the time. If I'd been in my right mind, I would've asked... why? I've never understood why. You were happy with Jayden. He was your whole world. Then, one day, BOOM. You leveled everything."

Darrel lifted one shoulder, unsure where to start. "You know me. I'm a dumbass."

Richie leaned back and took a swig of his beer before responding. "I'm not buying it."

A snort escaped Darrel. "No. Seriously. When it comes to Jayden, I'm a complete idiot. Every place we went, people would openly flirt with him—like I wasn't even there. It always pissed me off to no end, but I didn't want to be crazy, so I never said anything. I just swallowed it down. The jealousy built and grew, making me insane. I mean, you've seen Jayden."

"I have," Richie agreed. "It also hasn't escaped my notice he's fourteen years younger than you."

"Exactly," Darrel said. Richie obviously got it. "It's like it all exploded inside my head one day. Jayden didn't lose me. I lost myself." The storm calmed in Darrel's head, leaving him deflated. "Then, he was gone, and I realized the truth too late. He never would've left me or cheated on me.

That's not in Jayden's nature. He doesn't give up, and he cares more about other people than he does himself. Now I want my life back and it's too late."

"You're both still kicking. It's not too late."

A sardonic smile pulled at Darrel's lips at Richie's claim. He shook his head. "It feels pretty fucking over between us. Before the meds knocked him out tonight, I kissed him."

"Did he punch you in the balls?" Richie asked, sounding certain he already knew the answer.

"No, but to be fair, he can't see right now to aim for my balls."

A soft chuckle rumbled from Richie's chest. "Jayden is a spitfire. Trust me, his aim would've been dead on if he hadn't wanted that kiss."

Darrel wasn't so sure, but he let it go. After all, he kind of liked the idea that Jayden may have welcomed his touch. Hope was damn hard to stamp out when it came to Jayden. Darrel didn't know how to give up trying. For tonight, he had only one plan in mind—to get shitfaced. He didn't want to stumble from this bar. Darrel wanted someone to have to carry him out. In the morning, when he saw Jayden again, Darrel wanted his head to hurt so bad he couldn't possibly do anything else stupid. That was the only way he might make it through this life. Hell, if Jayden never took him back, maybe Darrel would stay drunk. Oblivion sounded damn good.

HE'D GOTTEN SO USED to Bryce being pressed against him in the bed, Jayden didn't react right away when Bryce tried waking him. "You've gotten lazy," Bryce said with a laugh, making Jayden wonder how long he'd been poking him in the ribs. "Dr. Vincent is here."

Jayden sucked in a hiss as he tried opening his eyes out of habit. The tearing sensation had him sucking air. "Fuck." Jayden dragged out the word, trying to stamp down the misery.

"Do you need something for the pain?"

The sound of Dr. Vincent's voice made Jayden realize what he'd said. "Sorry. I always have a second when I forget I shouldn't try opening my eyes when I wake up. It'll pass."

"I'll still order you something. Let's get something pumping through your system before I come back this afternoon and take your bandages off."

At the announcement, Jayden's brain stuttered to a stop. "You're taking the bandages off?"

"It's time," Dr. Vincent said, sounding confident. "After you asked me about your release last night, I thought things over. We should see how your vision is doing. At worst, we can replace your bandages and wait. At best, maybe you can go home soon where your friends will have an easier time caring for you. I have a few procedures scheduled for this morning, and then we'll get those off, get you cleaned up, and go from there. We'll start with an ultrasound and move to an eye exam. How does that sound?"

"Scary," Jayden said without a qualm.

"You've got this," Dr. Vincent said. "I'll be back later. Enjoy your breakfast, such as it is. It should still be hot. They just brought it in a few minutes ago."

Jayden nodded. "Okay."

"Your doctor is kind of hot," Bryce said quietly against his ear.

"Why are you whispering?" Jayden whispered back, in case Bryce had a good reason.

Bryce chuckled. "I don't know. Seemed like a dirty confession, considering he's taking care of you and I'm married. Plus, he might still be right outside the door."

Jayden smiled before a wave of sadness washed over him. "I miss your face. What if I never see it again?"

"Mhmm," Bryce hummed, sounding somewhat bitchy. "You're leaving me for San Diego, and now you miss my face."

Against his will, Jayden's smile was back. He snuggled closer to Bryce. "I have a confession."

"You have my attention."

Bryce's scandalous tone had Jayden feeling more like himself. "I don't think I want to go. Even if I can still see when this is over, and if they're even still willing to hire me after missing my start date, I'm not sure I want to move any longer."

"Really?" The note of confusion in Bryce's voice had Jayden telling all his secrets.

"When you took Richie back, I thought it might be best if I went away and let you have some time alone with him."

"Well, that's bullshit. I need you every bit as much as I need him."

Jayden nodded. He got it. Bryce was important to his existence too. "I could've died." Jayden choked on the last word and had to clear his throat.

Bryce ran his fingers through his hair, soothing him. "I don't want to run away."

"Are you running from me?" Bryce sounded calm, but Jayden knew him too well. He heard the hint of hurt beneath his words.

"You have a life. I fuck up everything I touch." He shrugged. "Maybe I should still go."

When Bryce spoke, his voice came out halted, as if he chose every word carefully. Jayden was dealing with the psychologist now. "You're my best friend. We've been there for each other in ways maybe some people wouldn't understand. But we get each other, you know? We're the kind of people who need affection in our lives, and we forgive people for things no one else would. Face it, Jayden. We're like two fucked-up peas in a pod."

"I agree with most of that, except for you being fucked up. You're perfect."

Bryce snorted. "Come on. You know that's not true. My parents didn't love me, so I turn to other people for fulfillment. Don't make me psychoanalyze myself. The point is, we need each other, and there's nothing you can do that would ever make me think badly of you. Richie knows me and accepts me as I am. You don't have to worry he'll ever tell me to stop loving up on you, because he knows I'm like an endless well of neediness." Bryce laughed, and added, "You don't ever have to worry about me thinking less of you if you want Darrel back either, because I'm pretty sure he'd rather die than hurt you again."

Jayden couldn't talk about Darrel. Not yet. "Richie doesn't know everything about us, I hope."

"What?" Bryce asked in the most innocent tone Jayden had ever heard. "Me not tell my husband something? Never. Of course he knows I've touched your dick. How could I resist such a young, gorgeous specimen? Besides, who else will help you pee?"

A snort of laughter escaped Jayden, forcing him to cover his nose and mouth. He swallowed down his chuckles and tried sounding serious for Bryce's sake. "And I don't think I can be blamed for attempting to seduce such a sexy man."

"Exactly," Bryce said, sounding as if he was having every bit as hard of a time not laughing. "I won't say you meant nothing, sexy, because that's not true. You mean everything."

Jayden's cheeks hurt from smiling. "I love you. Now tell me about this doctor. I bring patients here all the time, but I can't place him. The name doesn't ring any bells."

Bryce pressed several noisy kisses on Jayden's neck before settling back down. "I love you too. Okay," Bryce said, snuggling close. "He's about six-two. Blond and about my age."

"Mhmm. You know I love older men."

"I do know it. We have experience and stamina. Oh, he has dark blue eyes and a nice smile."

"Wait," Jayden said, interrupting. "I know who he is. He's only been here about a month or so. The hospital assigned me to his care because I never go to the doctor and don't have one. Tiffany tried flirting with him once when we were dropping off a patient. It didn't go well. Sheesh, all you hot men surrounding me, and not a single eye for me to use."

"Luckily, God blessed you with two working hands."

Another bark of laughter escaped Jayden before he could call it back.

"Are you having a party in here?"

There was a time when Jayden's smile would have fallen at Darrel's appearance. Jayden very much feared, this time, his smile grew. Damn, he missed his eyesight. Darrel was a gorgeous man with his dark skin and sexy light-brown eyes. His lips made Jayden hot. Maybe it was a good thing he couldn't see. Darrel was bad for his heart.

"Jayden was telling me a story about Tiffany," Bryce lied without hesitation.

"It's good to hear you laughing," Darrel said, moving to the side of Jayden's bed. Jayden followed the sound of his voice. "Speaking of Tiffany," Darrel added. "She's stopped by a few times to check on you, but you've been asleep every time."

"I'll call her," Jayden said before he remembered he couldn't see and his phone was dead. "If someone will charge my phone and find her number in my contacts. Fuck if I know anyone's number by heart."

"You might want to wait for a decent time," Darrel said with a laugh. Jayden's smile grew at the sound. Damn, he was stupid. Sometimes Jayden wondered if he liked having people ruin his life.

"Not being able to see is really fucking with my internal clock. I have no idea what time it is."

"It's six a.m.," Darrel said.

Jayden held tighter to Bryce. "Damn. We slept all night. I'm surprised Richie didn't kick the door in and drag you home."

"Nah," Darrel said, snagging Jayden's attention. "He was with me."

"Yep," Bryce said, sounding cheerful. "They had a man date while we had our slumber party."

Jayden nodded. He missed man dates and being part of the group. Back when Richie left Bryce, Jayden had made a conscious decision to break from their group of friends and stick with Bryce. Like it or not, friends took sides when buddies split. He'd chosen Bryce and not looked back. As far as Jayden was concerned, he got the best of the bunch. Now Richie and Bryce were not only back together but married. Jayden still didn't feel like part of the crowd. "Did we miss anything good?"

"Lots of heavy drinking," Darrel said with a laugh.

"Then I didn't miss anything." Jayden wasn't much of a drinker and they were pumping him full of the good drugs.

"We missed you," Darrel said quietly. The words sounded sincere enough that Jayden's breath caught.

Bryce slid from the bed. "I guess I should run home and make sure Richie lived through the night. He doesn't drink much anymore."

"Sure," Jayden said, dragging out the word. "That's why you're rushing home."

Bryce pressed a quick kiss to the corner of

Jayden's mouth and dropped his voice to a stage whisper. "You're right. He's twice as kinky when he's drunk. I'm not missing that."

Darrel's low chuckle rumbled through the room and caused chill bumps to break out on Jayden's skin. "You'd better hurry, then. He's likely to sober up soon."

"I'll be back this afternoon before the doctor makes his rounds," Bryce promised.

The room fell silent. Since Jayden couldn't see, the quiet felt twice as uncomfortable. He cleared his throat and tried to think of something to say. Nothing came to mind.

Darrel came to the rescue. "Has the doctor been in already this morning?"

Jayden nodded. "You just missed him. Bryce says he's hot. Is that why you keep coming around?" God help him. The question was out there, hanging in the universe before Jayden could stop it. The hush that fell in the aftermath of his question had Jayden wishing he could take it back. The lull lasted for long enough Jayden wondered if Darrel left. He wouldn't blame the man if he did. Getting cheated on, that was a damn hard thing to let go.

After what seemed like forever, Darrel finally spoke. "If I was in that bed, you'd be here. That's who you are. You care more about others than you do yourself. That's why I'm here."

"Sorry. I—"

"I'm also here because I love you," Darrel said, cutting off his apology. "But that doesn't matter."

"It matters to me."

"What did the doctor say?" Darrel asked, obviously determined to change the subject.

Jayden blew out a breath. There was no sense in pushing things. "Later today, they'll ultrasound my eyes to look closer at the damage. Afterward, we'll test how much I can see, if at all." Jayden's words came out shaky. He wanted to get it over with. Then again, if he couldn't see, he'd know, and there was no unlearning that.

"You still have a lot of healing to do," Darrel said, sounding sure of every word leaving his lips. "No matter what happens today, you still have better days ahead."

Jayden turned away from the sound of his voice. He didn't know—with most of his face covered— how much Darrel could glean from his expressions. Jayden didn't want to take any chances. Everyone had blown smoke up his ass from the moment he'd awoken in this place. He'd hoped, considering Darrel had never cared about his feelings before, maybe he would be at least a little forthright. It seemed insane to need one person who freaked the fuck out alongside him, but there it was. Jayden wanted someone to commiserate with him. Instead, everyone was so goddamn positive, and it all felt fake.

The more he thought about things, the darker his thoughts got until a growl escaped him. "I wish, for once, someone would just fucking acknowledge that I might not ever see again."

"No one believes that," Darrel said, sounding calm and doing nothing to help Jayden's temper.

"I don't care what anyone believes," Jayden snapped, completely losing his temper. "There's a chance that I'll never see again. If that happens, I don't know what I'll do, but for fuck's sake, please stop placating me." Jayden's voice rose with each word until he was practically yelling.

"Fine," Darrel snapped back. "If you need to talk about what'll happen if you can't see, we'll talk about it. If you can't see, Bryce will take you home with him and baby you. You'll never want for a thing, and you'll never have to look at my cheating face again while remembering how I fucked up your life. Do you feel better now?"

A snort escaped Jayden, followed by a laugh.

He'd never been good at holding on to his temper. "Oddly, yes."

"Well, I don't," Darrel grumbled. "Do you want me to feed you breakfast before it gets cold?"

"I want you to not be angry anymore," Jayden answered, his smile slipping away. He needed Darrel to find happiness again even if it wasn't with him. Maybe then, Jayden could find peace.

"Well, that's not going to happen," Darrel said. The sound of the tray rattling closer filled the air. "As long as I live, I plan to be mad as hell at myself, and there's not a damn thing you can do to stop that."

Jayden's chest ached. "I want to be friends."

"You have pancakes, bacon, and coffee. They really do act like syrup is coming out their checks around here. I don't know if I can be only your friend, baby," Darrel said, floundering between topics.

"Then why are you here?"

"Because I am your fucking friend," Darrel snapped. Jayden jumped as the silverware rattled as if Darrel had slammed something down on the tray.

Jayden chewed on his bottom lip. He didn't want to fight. "Maybe you should go do something else. I think you're getting burned out, being here with me."

Without a word, Darrel helped Jayden find his food. He was getting pretty good at feeding himself without being able to see what he was doing. Before Jayden could take a bite, he found his head pressed back against the bed and Darrel's mouth covering his. There was nothing passionate about it. Their tongues didn't meet. Jayden was too shocked to make a move. Darrel's kiss lightened until their lips barely brushed. The man's soft lips stroked his once more.

"Eat. I'll be back later."

The sound of the room door closing followed Darrel's words. Like that, Jayden was alone for the first time since he'd awoken in the hospital. He didn't know if he was relieved or panicked. For the most part, Jayden just hurt.

DARREL DIDN'T GO FAR. He was scared shitless that Jayden would need him. What if he spilled his coffee? It was still hot. Fuck. Mostly, he was overly tired. Darrel had been spending every day without fail at Jayden's bedside so Bryce could work. When

Bryce got there, Darrel caught a few hours of sleep, then headed off to third shift, since he'd talked a buddy into switching shifts with him until Jayden was better. Even though he was used to running on little to no sleep, adding the stress of everything on top of being exhausted had life kicking his ass.

After opening the door a crack so he could keep an eye on Jayden, Darrel sat down in the hallway. Everything he did was wrong. Sometimes, he thought about disappearing. He could drive across the country and start a new life somewhere. No one would know about the mistakes he'd made. The only thing stopping him was feet away in a hospital bed.

Darrel turned his head and eyed Jayden. He wasn't eating. The man sat, head bowed over his tray, and unmoving. Darrel's eyes fell closed. He needed to do something useful. Jayden had been without a cellphone since the explosion. It had gone dead shortly after he'd been admitted, and everyone kept forgetting to bring a charger. After pushing to his feet, Darrel checked on Jayden through the crack. He still wasn't doing anything. Darrel's chest ached and his throat swelled. He turned away before he could burst through the door and do more damage.

Instead, he headed for his truck. Every step, moving away from Jayden, was hell. But today, he could do more good away from Jayden than with him. Since Jayden had a different phone from him, Darrel ran to the store and bought a new cord. While there, he grabbed the man some of his favorite snacks. At the last minute, he snagged a stuffed frog and added it to the mix. Once he was back inside his truck, Darrel didn't leave. He couldn't go back to the hospital. Not yet. The more time they spent together, the harder things got. Jayden was getting better. All Darrel's sins were rearing their heads again now that Jayden didn't really need him any longer.

He dug his phone out and scrolled through his social media accounts, killing time. Before he realized it would happen, Darrel found himself staring at a picture of Jayden and him on the beach. He'd driven all night while Jayden slept to get them there. It had been a last-minute idea. He'd wanted to do something for Jayden no one else ever had. They'd spent a week holed up in a room directly on the beach. Everything had been perfect about that week, including the moment when Darrel had found himself dropping to one knee. Jayden had looked at him like he was insane. Darrel had never been more terrified. If Jayden had turned him down, nothing would've changed, but Darrel would've known he wasn't good enough to marry. But Jayden had said yes, and Darrel had gone on to prove he really wasn't good enough to marry.

With no real plan, Darrel scrolled through his contacts and pulled up Jayden's number. All their past messages were still there. The transformation from love to hate was an obvious date on the calendar. He touched the bubble to send a new message. Jayden wouldn't get it until he charged his phone. In fact, without his eyesight, Darrel could delete it before Jayden knew it existed. With that plan firmly in place, Darrel started typing. He didn't hold back a single thought. It was way past time for him to say everything he needed to say.

Darrel: *I've never been a good man. Not before you, during you, or after you left. When we met, you were dating Wyatt. I told myself you were better off with him. He's a great guy. And still, I went home after every time I saw you, wishing you were mine and dreaming you'd look at me just once the way you looked at him. Then, you were single, and I told myself to give you space. I lie a lot to myself, but the biggest lie I ever told was that I could let go of the fantasy of you. The crazy thing is—I never really fantasized about the sex, which I do miss like crazy, but fuck if I'm touching* anyone else, because I belong to you. Every time I thought about having you, it was always kissing you. Holding you. Linking my fingers through yours and hanging on.

Then, one night, you turned up on my doorstep. You looked at me the way I always hoped you would. It happened without me having to do a thing. You found me on your own. I thought I'd won the damn lottery. Like most lottery winners, I threw it all away. Not because I didn't love you, but because I more than love you. You're an obsession. A crazed mind will take you down a million roads. Each one darker than the last. Every time someone flirted with you, and everyone flirts with you. Jesus. Men and women, it doesn't matter. Everyone takes one look at you, and they're in your pocket. My fucked-up brain had a field day with that. The more I fixated upon you, the tighter I held on. The harder I clung, the more everything unraveled inside my head. Every day, I became more and more certain you'd find someone better. Because, hell, everyone is better than me. What I did to you, it wasn't weakness. I wasn't tempted away. There's no one out there who can upstage you or touch my heart. It was crazed obsession, making me see problems that weren't there. I had to destroy myself, so I could rebuild myself better. Loving you, that hasn't changed. You're the one for me, even if we're never together again. I'm not saying, if you don't take me back, I'll never date again. Maybe I will someday, but my heart will always know what it's missing. You're the strongest person I *know. You'll be fine no matter what. You can get past these injuries, and you can survive me. But I haven't survived you. Not really. To be honest, I don't want to, because I need the world to see I kept my unspoken vow to love you until death do we part.*

Darrel hit send and set his phone aside. No one else would ever know what he'd admitted, but he would. Darrel would always know.

JAYDEN SPENT the whole day alone, and it was hell. He fought to find the button to call the nurse each and every time he needed to use the restroom or do anything. Having someone stay with him all day had spoiled him. Not being able to see, worrying over whether he'd be able to see again, and every fucking thing about Darrel had shot Jayden's mood to hell. He was over everything and wanted to go home.

"Are you ready to do this?" Dr. Vincent asked, sailing into the room and bringing Jayden's inner raging to a halt.

Jayden jumped in surprise. He'd been alone all day, and every noise startled him. He was damn ready to see again. "As ready as I'll ever be, I suppose."

"Let's start slow," Dr. Vincent said, lowering the railing and sitting on the edge of the bed. "I'm leaving the lights off in here. If you can see, hopefully having only the sunlight filtering into the room will keep your pain level low. We'll add more light as we go."

Jayden nodded. "Okay."

"Keep your eyes closed."

Jayden did as Dr. Vincent ordered. It wasn't hard since it hurt too badly to open them. "All right."

The tape pulled at Jayden's skin as the doctor removed the gauze and bandages. Cool air brushed his burns, forcing a hiss from his lips.

"It'll get better. Keep your eyes closed. I want to treat these wounds before looking at your eyes."

"Okay," Jayden mumbled while trying to hold still.

A cool cream coated his skin. It stung before going numb. "Now you'll feel something wet dripping on your lashes. I'm just cleaning everything to make it easier for you to open your eyes. Are you doing okay?"

Jayden flashed the man a smile. "So far, so good."

Cool liquid splashed his closed lids before the doctor swiped at them. Between the topical medicine and the pain meds, Jayden's discomfort was minimal.

Dr. Vincent took a breath, sounding every bit as nervous as Jayden felt. "Okay. Let's give it a go. Try opening your eyes."

Jayden expected his eyes to pop right open upon command. Instead, he had to work at it, as if his lashes were stuck. Then, the room came into view —sort of. Everything was hazy—like he was in desperate need of glasses. He winced against the light assaulting his eyes, even though it wasn't bright.

"Can you see anything?"

"A little." Even Jayden heard the disappointment in his voice. His chest hurt. He wasn't completely blind, but neither could he see. Not really.

"Let me put some eye drops in your eyes and get some natural moisture building and clean away any loose debris. That might help some."

Jayden dutifully tilted his head back and let the doctor do his thing. The eye drops burned like acid hit his eyes. Jayden sucked in a breath and held it. After blinking a few times, the doctor's face became clearer. His sight wasn't perfect. He could only make out shapes of objects if they weren't inches from his face, but it beat blindness. The guy had nice eyes. He looked kind.

"What's your first name?"

The man's gaze shifted from what his hands were doing to Jayden's eyes. "Bay."

A smile pulled at Jayden's lips. "That's the most un-doctorly name I've ever heard, but it's a good name."

Bay smiled, and Jayden's shoulders relaxed. He looked nice. Like people liked him. "Thank you. Although, I admit, it was a better name before all the kids started calling their girlfriends and boyfriends that."

A chuckle escaped Jayden. "I didn't even think about that. I can see your face."

A bright smile touched the man's features. "That's great. Anything else?"

Jayden glanced around and shook his head. "Everything else is mostly a blur."

"It's a start. Here," he said, pushing something cold into Jayden's hands. "I know, if I was in your place, I'd want to know the damage. Take a look."

Jayden realized it was a mirror. He brought the round glass as close as possible to his face and inspected the wounds. It wasn't terrible. He'd probably look like hell for a little while, but nothing appeared bad enough to scar, except his chin and neck. His hair stood in every direction and badly needed a brush. "Oh, lord. I'm a hot mess."

Bay reclaimed the mirror. "You're definitely one of those things," he said under his breath, making Jayden wonder if he'd heard right. "Now here's a question for you," Bay continued as if nothing happened. "Do you want to re-bandage your wounds and try again in a few days, or do you want to leave them uncovered and see if things get better with practice?"

Jayden didn't want to go back to seeing nothing, but his eyes hurt. "Which do you think is best?"

Bay stayed quiet for a moment as if thinking things over before answering. "I think, if we start you on an eye drop routine and you can stand it, you should go ahead with keeping them uncovered. If you're in pain, close your eyes and take breaks. Otherwise, look around. See if things improve."

"Oh my god. I can see your beautiful face," Bryce said, his voice filling the room. "Tell me everything."

Two shadowy figures filled the doorway. "I can only see things really close to my face." Even Jayden was surprised by how accepting he sounded.

"Lucky for me, I love being close to you."

Bay smiled and stood from where he sat perched on the edge of Jayden's bed. "I'm optimistic he'll make a full recovery."

Jayden's smile grew at the claim. "Let's do as you suggested and leave the bandages off. Bryce is my best friend," Jayden explained. For some reason, he wanted the doctor to know he was single. "I've missed his face and want to see him."

"I'll leave you to it, then, and I'll check back with you later."

"Thank you." Jayden sounded every bit as sincere as he felt. As the doctor's shape disappeared, Bryce took his place. Then, the man's gorgeous eyes came into view and Jayden fought the urge to cry. His throat swelled, and his eyes burned. He blinked, swallowing the sensations. "There you are." Jayden's words came out in a whisper.

"If I was witnessing this exchange with anyone else, I'd be jealous," Richie said with a chuckle, making Jayden realize he was the second shadowy figure. "Where's Darrel?"

"I'm here," Darrel said, coming through the

door. "Hey," he said, his voice turning bright. "I can see your gorgeous eyes. What's the verdict?"

"What's in the bag?" Jayden asked, rather than answering.

"Oh my god. You can see."

Jayden chuckled. "No. I can hear the plastic rattling. But," he said before Darrel got the wrong impression, "I can make out your outline. And," he added, getting excited despite not being able to see as well as he hoped, "if you come sit where Bryce is, I can see you."

Bryce stood, making room for Darrel. Jayden held his breath. Darrel's weight joined him on the bed, and then the man's face came into view. He looked tired. It didn't matter. Darrel was still the most gorgeous man on the planet. Jayden's eyes burned. He no longer knew if it was from the injuries or unshed tears.

"It's good to see you." Jayden's voice betrayed him. It held all his pain.

"Is it?"

Jayden pressed his lips together for a moment, fighting off his irritation. "You're really determined to fight today, aren't you?"

Darrel's eyes fell closed, stealing the man's gorgeous stare from him. When they reopened, his eyes were filled with regret. "I bought you some stuff. It's mostly just snacks, but I also brought a cord so you can finally charge your phone, and this," he said, pulling something from the bag. Darrel pressed it into his hand.

It was soft. Jayden brought it to his face and peered closer. A green stuffed frog with huge plastic eyes stared back at him. His irritation slipped away. "He has big brown eyes. Just like you." Jayden held him to his chest. "Thank you."

Something dark passed over Darrel's features and he looked away. "I just wanted to bring this stuff by before I go to work."

Jayden nodded. He already knew in his heart this would be Darrel's last visit to the hospital. They knew now Jayden wouldn't be there much longer. Darrel's duty to him was done. "Thank you. For everything," Jayden tacked on. Since Darrel wouldn't be back, Jayden needed to get his thanks in now.

"You got this," Darrel said, coming to his feet. He leaned in and pressed a light kiss on the corner of Jayden's mouth. For a moment, Jayden pressed closer, trying to hang on to what little he still he had of Darrel. Then Darrel straightened away and was gone.

Even without his full eyesight, the discomfort in the room was evident. Bryce scrambled to move them past it. "Let's plug your phone in. I bet you've got a thousand and one messages."

Jayden nodded absently. His mind still with Darrel. "Just mute them. I'll catch up reading them when it doesn't hurt so bad." Even Jayden didn't know if he meant his eyes or his heart.

CHAPTER 5

THE FOLLOW-UP APPOINTMENTS WERE KICKING Jayden in the ass and in the pride. His heart wasn't making out so well either. He'd gotten close to fifty percent of his eyesight back since his release. Jayden knew he should be grateful to have that much. It was damn hard when the doctors were speculating this was the best he'd ever be. That meant no more doing the job he loved. It meant a million things he couldn't look too closely at or he'd break.

"How do you feel about meeting Darrel for lunch at the diner?"

Darrel was Richie's best friend. The last thing Jayden wanted was to come between them. It was bad enough Richie was stuck having to take Jayden to every doctor's appointment, since it looked like Jayden would never drive again. "You should go ahead. I'm sure Darrel would love that. I can take a cab home."

An odd mixture of emotions crossed Richie's face before landing on confused. "I'm equally sure Darrel would love you being there as well, so what am I missing?"

Jayden tried choosing his words carefully. He didn't want to start anything. "I've been out three weeks and I haven't seen or heard from Darrel since the day he raced from my hospital room. You saw it. He full-on ran for his life. My guess is, whatever drove him to stay with me as long as he did at the hospital has passed since it's obvious I'll be fine. It's okay. I understand. I'm the ex. If he doesn't want to see me, I shouldn't thrust my company on him."

A long, loud sigh escaped Richie. "I shouldn't do this. It feels too much like I'm betraying a friend."

"Then you shouldn't do it," Jayden said, cutting him off. "I'm glad we're friends again, and I don't want to ruin that."

"But," Richie said over the top of him, "Darrel gave me some good advice when I was trying to win Bryce back, so I'll help him however I can. He loves you."

Jayden blinked. "I know. That doesn't mean he's

not done with me. People walk away from people they love all the time, especially when they're saving themselves."

"Would you be quiet and listen?" Richie said, unlocking the passenger side door and opening it for Jayden.

Jayden fought back a smile as he pretended to zip his lips and throw away the key.

Richie shook his head as he closed Jayden inside the car. He didn't speak again until he was behind the wheel. "You're going to lunch with us because I know Darrel. He won't call or come see you until you make the first move. Darrel knows everything between the two of you is his fault. He thinks you want him out of your life. Before the bank robbery, I would've agreed. Now, I don't think that's true."

Jayden couldn't argue with that assumption. Also, he'd zipped his lips.

Richie sighed like the put-upon man he was. "You can speak."

A chuckle escaped Jayden. He didn't know why he liked fucking with Richie so much. Maybe because the man needed a little humor in his life. "I have no problem going to lunch with Darrel. All I said was I shouldn't thrust my company upon him if he doesn't want it. Since you're his best friend, and you would know, if you say he won't be mad about me being there, then that's all I needed to know."

"Jesus," Richie breathed, keeping his gaze locked on the road. "I feel like Bryce is teaching a course on how to get under my skin. But when?" he asked, as if talking to himself. "I don't give him that much space. In fact, I'd go so far as to say I'm always up his ass."

A burst of laughter escaped Jayden. "Oh, god. Stop."

Richie flashed him a smile. "We like having you around."

A lump formed in his throat. Jayden gave the man's arm a pat. "You always say the right thing at the right time."

Before Jayden's eyes, Richie turned serious. "I remember what it was like, coming home from the hospital and finding myself dependent on everyone else for all the things I'd been doing alone for most my life. Swallowing your pride is a lot fucking harder than people will give you credit for, so I don't want you to think of it like that. Bryce and I want you with us. Okay?"

"You're a good man, Richie, and you're doing an amazing job of distracting me from the fact I'll be seeing Darrel soon. We should ask Bryce if he wants to join us too."

A soft chuckle filled the car. Richie turned in to the parking lot of the diner. "He's got a twelve o'clock appointment. Don't change the subject. I know I'm not very suave. So I'll tell it like it is," he said, shifting into park. "Darrel loves you. You love him. Eventually, you'll both have to face that. Otherwise, neither of you will ever move on." Richie's gaze moved past Jayden and fixed on the window a half second before Jayden's door opened.

Jayden dropped his gaze to the hand that appeared in front of him. He followed the dark arm until his gaze met light-brown eyes that caused his heart to skip a beat. Damn. Richie was right. He was still in love with Darrel Johnson. Darrel's serious expression made Jayden wonder at his thoughts. He set his hand in Darrel's. Darrel tugged, helping him from the car.

"I didn't know you were joining us, but I'm glad to see you out and about."

Jayden swallowed back the words crowding his throat. "Richie took me to my doctor's appointment today. It ran longer than expected, spilling over into your lunch plans."

"I'm glad you came." Darrel's gaze moved over

Jayden's face at the claim, as if calculating Jayden's every reaction.

"Me too," Jayden said. A chuckle escaped him as he realized he hadn't let go of Darrel's hand. He didn't miss the flash of disappointment that crossed Darrel's features when he did.

Since both Richie and Darrel had ordered the wrap, their food came first. "Damn," Jayden cursed. "Everyone always gets their food before me."

Richie chuckled. "When we close on the new house and have our dream kitchen, I might let you cook some nights, then no one can stop you from serving yourself first."

Darrel looked between Richie and Jayden, wearing an unreadable expression. "I thought you were moving to San Diego."

Jayden tried not meeting Darrel's gorgeous gaze. He didn't want the man to see his feelings. "I was, but after thinking things over and discussing some things with Bryce and Richie, I've decided to stay." Jayden snatched a fry from Richie's plate.

Richie huffed. "Damn. I already let you kiss my husband. Now you want my fries too."

"You can have one of mine when my food gets here. If I ever get a husband, I'll let you kiss him if you want." Jayden accidentally caught Darrel's eye as he made the claim. An unexpected blush raced to his cheeks. His gaze skirted away.

"Sorry I'm late," Bryce said, appearing at the edge of the table and distracting Jayden.

Happiness exploded through Jayden, wiping away his discomfort. "I didn't think you were coming. Richie said you had an appointment."

Bryce kissed his cheek as Jayden slid from the booth, letting the man sit next to his husband. "My twelve o'clock rescheduled."

Without thought, Jayden slid in next to Darrel.

"Hey, sexy," Richie said, capturing Bryce's lips like he hadn't seen the man in days rather than hours.

Jayden wanted to look away, but he couldn't. He loved seeing Bryce happy. The pair gave him hope.

"If you're not going to San Diego, are you back to work?" Darrel asked, pulling Jayden's gaze his way.

Darrel's arm was slung across the back of the seat. Jayden had a hard time focusing on anything other than how close Darrel sat—like they were together. "Not yet. I'm in an odd position, because the day I got hurt was supposed to be my last day. Not to mention, I'd given notice at my duplex. Things are sort of up in the air."

"Are you okay? Do you need a place to stay?" The concern in Darrel's eyes warmed Jayden's heart.

Richie answered before Jayden got the chance. "We've got him. Last weekend, we moved him into our guest bedroom. Once we're in our new place, he can stay in the guest house. It'll work out perfectly for everyone."

"He's working as my medical assistant for now," Bryce added, stealing food from Richie's plate. "At least until his eyesight is better, or for as long as he wants. I'd be happy for him to keep at it, since I need him," Bryce said as he shoved two fries in his mouth.

Darrel looked between them. "You should've said something. I would've helped you move."

"We assumed you were busy," Richie answered for him again, making Jayden wonder why everyone thought he was incapable of speaking for himself.

Darrel focused on Jayden. "I'm never too busy for you."

The air thickened. Someone was finally looking at him for a response, and Jayden had nothing. Darrel was too close. Jayden's gaze dropped to the lips he missed before snapping back to Darrel's eyes when he realized what he'd done. "I'll keep that in mind." He looked away before he embarrassed himself further. Bryce's knowing smile had Jayden blushing again.

A plate appeared in front of him, saving Jayden from himself. He'd never felt awkward around Darrel before. Jayden had no clue why he did now. Perhaps it had something to do with the way the man smelled. Delicious. Or maybe, Jayden was just an idiot.

DARREL COULDN'T STOP STARING at Jayden. He needed a haircut. The temptation to run his fingers through Jayden's soft brown hair was real. His palms itched from the need. Jayden had blushed twice in the short time he'd been there. Since Jayden wasn't the blushing type, Darrel was fascinated. Of course, Darrel was always intrigued by Jayden. Before Jayden had finally agreed to date him, Darrel had spent countless hours each time they were out as a group staring at Jayden. He'd memorized the man's every nuance. Darrel was there again, intently watching Jayden's every move and wishing the man would look his way. Instead, Jayden kept his gaze locked on his plate. He didn't say a word while Bryce and Richie chatted happily.

A shadow fell over the table, snagging Darrel's attention. A tall and slender blond man with dark blue eyes, wearing jeans and a button-down shirt, hovered at Jayden's side. While wearing street clothes, it took Darrel a minute to place him. The table fell silent. Bryce was the first one who spoke.

"Dr. Vincent. It's nice to see you."

He nodded but didn't smile. Darrel marveled over how, even without smiling, the man looked friendly. It was like he bled congeniality. "Dr. Tuthill. It's good to see you again as well." The man's gaze moved Jayden's way and his features shifted. Suddenly, the man didn't seem quite as nice. Darrel had all sorts of warning bells ringing in his head. "Jayden. How are you?"

Jayden's dimples showed. Darrel wanted to hit something. "I'm doing okay. How about you?"

While eyeing Jayden like he inspected Jayden's injuries, the doctor nodded. "I can't complain. Just finished having lunch with my sister," he said, motioning toward a slender woman who was headed for the door. "If you have a minute, I'd like to discuss something with you." He cast a glance around the table, adding, "If that's all right with your friends, of course."

Bryce answered for everyone, before Darrel had time to shut this shit down. "We don't mind at all." His tone said he knew each and every one of Darrel's fears, and they were all true. "Jayden, go talk with the man."

It was the first time Darrel ever wanted to punch Bryce in his perfect teeth. Jayden slid from the booth, giving Darrel something else to concentrate on. Darrel watched him head outside with the doctor. Fuck. The man was a doctor. Darrel couldn't compete with that, especially when added with Darrel's past transgressions. He didn't stand a chance. Darrel's gaze slid to the window. After shifting an inch to the right, he had an okayish view of the pair standing on the sidewalk. The man shuffled nearer. Jayden didn't step back. As Darrel looked on, the man moved even closer and inspected Jayden's eyes. His actions mimicked a doctor's. The dude's posture screamed more. He wanted Jayden. It was in the good doctor's every line. The guy was half a second away from pouncing. Jayden didn't look opposed. Goddamn it.

"Quit staring at Jayden and Bay. Jayden might start to think you care."

At Richie's claim, Darrel tore his gaze away and focused on his friend. Each breath he took came harder than the last. "What? How long have they been dating?"

Richie looked up from his plate. A deep line formed between his eyebrows. "What? Nobody said anything about them dating."

"You said, 'Jayden and his bae.'"

The confusion written on Richie's face might've been funny if Darrel's heart wasn't crumbling inside his chest. "When the fuck have you ever heard me use the word 'bae'? I said, 'Jayden and Bay.' The dude's name is literally Bay."

Darrel switched his gaze between Richie and Bryce, looking for any signs the guy was fucking with him. Richie's face was clear of all emotion while Bryce seemed a bit too triumphant for Darrel's taste. He found himself risking a limb by snapping at Bryce, "Quit looking so goddamn happy. I know you're getting what you want right now."

Richie growled. Full on—like a wild animal ready to attack. "Don't fucking talk to him like that."

Darrel's chest hurt. He didn't want this. These were his friends.

"It's okay," Bryce said, patting Richie's arm and before Darrel could apologize. "I'd be the same if I thought I was about to lose you to someone else." He focused all his attention on Darrel. "Rather than snapping at me, you should try manning the fuck up."

"Yeah," Richie said, having his husband's back.

Bryce wasn't finished. "Jayden has a heart of gold. I'd stake money that he's forgiven you, even though you don't deserve it. It's all up to you at this point."

"We're just friends now." Even to Darrel's ears, it sounded like a lie. Still, he'd decided. Jayden deserved better than him, and that was what Jayden would get. Fuck all. A doctor was better than him, even if the guy had a stupid name.

Jayden reappeared, saving Darrel from Bryce's retort. "Wow. No one ate my food. That has to be a first."

"You need to get your strength back," Richie said, concentrating on his plate. "What did Bay want?" Richie asked before Jayden's ass even hit the bench next to Darrel.

Jayden shrugged and ate a fry. "He asked me about how things are going with my new primary care physician."

"That's good," Bryce said between bites of Richie's food. "The man obviously cares about his former patients."

"Then he asked me out," Jayden added, punching Darrel in the throat with his words.

Darrel dropped his gaze to his half-eaten turkey wrap. He couldn't hide his reaction. Luckily, Jayden didn't look his way.

"Whoa. Really?" Bryce asked, sounding excited before swiftly transforming into the expressionless psychologist. "You can tell me all about it later."

Jayden took a bite of his burger and swallowed before responding again. "It's no big deal. I gave him my number and told him I'd think about it. My life is kind of in shambles right now. I'm hardly a catch at the moment."

"What kind of bullshit is that?" Darrel asked before he could stop himself, so he didn't try. "Anyone who doesn't recognize they're lucky as fuck to have a shot at you is too dumb to live."

Jayden glanced over and met his gaze. Darrel couldn't look away. "Thanks, but I don't want to start anything with anyone when I've got nothing to offer. I can't get anyone to fall in love with me when I'm on equal footing. The last thing I need is to fall for anyone else who finds me lacking while I really am lacking. My ego can't take the blow."

Every time Darrel thought he couldn't hate himself more, he found a new low. Not only did he love Jayden, the man had been his friend before Darrel destroyed his life. He was a bastard. Everyone knew it. Jayden's leg pressed against his, crowding Darrel beneath the table, and easing the tightness in his chest. Darrel knew he should move away. Sitting like this didn't fit with Darrel's plan to leave Jayden be and let him find happiness. Darrel was paralyzed. The heat of Jayden's skin against his rendered Darrel useless. Jayden kept eating. If he noticed Darrel's struggle, he didn't let on.

Darrel decided to pretend he didn't notice either, but he couldn't keep talking about Jayden and the doctor. "Did you have to take apart that glass shelf case thingie with all the tiny screws to move it?" he asked the table in general, going back to the discussion of Jayden moving in with Bryce and letting go of the topic of Jayden dating.

Everyone groaned, but Bryce answered, "There's no good way to move that damn thing, but it's Grammie's, so," he said, shrugging.

Jayden chuckled. "It's still sitting in a pile of

pieces in my bedroom. None of us have worked up the fortitude to put all the tiny screws in again."

"I'll come do it," Darrel offered without thought. Once it was out there, he didn't take it back. "After moving it twice already, you know I've become the expert at assembly."

Jayden's gorgeous green gaze moved over his face. A warmth spread through Darrel's chest. "Are you sure?"

Darrel shrugged. "Absolutely. Today's my day off. I can take you home from here and have it together in no time."

A slow smile spread across Jayden's face. Darrel fought the urge to scoot closer. He'd never wanted to kiss anyone as badly. "I'd love you forever. You know Grammie would kill me if I got rid of that case, but it's a huge pain."

He wanted Jayden to love him forever. Fuck. Why couldn't he just walk away? A good man would stop this now. "I don't mind at all." It seemed Darrel wasn't a good man after all.

WHILE SITTING on the floor with his back leaned against his bed, Jayden watched Darrel gathering all the pieces for the shelves. Darrel could feel the man's gaze burrowing into his skin. It took every ounce of his self-control to stop himself from pouncing. They were too close. The bedroom wasn't that big.

"You know, it's just occurred to me. Every time I've put this together, I've used that one screwdriver in that specialty toolkit you bought me for Christmas three years ago. If I don't run home and get it, I won't be able to do this today. You want to ride with me?" Please, God. He needed to get the fuck out of there and get some air.

Jayden dropped his gaze to his hands. He wasn't quick enough to hide his wince. "I don't like going to your house." Despite keeping his face averted, Darrel didn't miss the way Jayden's face screwed up in pain. "Sorry. I don't know why I said that."

Darrel knew. That was where they'd lost everything. Where Darrel had ruined Jayden's life. He moved without thought. While keeping his weight braced on his knees, Darrel straddled Jayden's lap. Jayden flattened his hands against Darrel's chest, as if he thought to push him away. Darrel snagged Jayden's wrists and gently urged Jayden's hands above his head until he held them braced against the mattress behind them.

Jayden tilted his chin up. Their gazes met. Darrel lowered his head. Jayden didn't turn away. The moment their lips met, passion exploded through their kiss. Their tongues stroked and retreated, searching for more. Darrel couldn't stop pressing harder against Jayden until they'd shifted positions, and he had Jayden pinned to the floor. The instant Jayden's hands were free, he reached for the button on Darrel's pants. Darrel blocked him. This wasn't about him. Hell, it wasn't even about sex. Not really. There was just so much love inside Darrel for this man. It had nowhere to go and had been ignored for too long. He didn't want to ruin Jayden's life anymore. Darrel only wanted to do good things for the man beneath him. He needed to make Jayden smile again. Being trapped with Jayden, this close to the man's bed when there was so much hunger in Darrel's heart, he couldn't stop himself from tasting Jayden. He needed this.

Darrel's fingers found the edge of Jayden's soft V-neck t-shirt. He eased the material up, baring the man's flat stomach and the line of dark hair that disappeared inside the his ripped jeans. Darrel's lips moved down Jayden's body. He needed to feel Jayden's soft stomach against his lips. The light-colored jeans Jayden wore had several holes, showing off the man's naturally bronzed skin. Darrel's gaze had slid down Jayden's body, taking in the vision more than once today. Now he worked down the zipper of those jeans that taunted him as his kissed the spot below Jayden's navel. Darrel set Jayden's erection free. Every muscle in his body tightened as he caught sight of Jayden's gorgeous dick. Damn, this was the only man who'd ever sent him up in flames from just a glimpse of his nudity. Jayden cupped Darrel's shaved head. Darrel's gaze flew to Jayden's. The uncertainty in Jayden's eyes had Darrel lowering his chin. He dragged his tongue down Jayden's length while holding the man's stare. Jayden's lips parted on a pant. A flush tinted his cheeks. Darrel licked his way back to Jayden's crown and swallowed the man's cock.

A moan vibrated from the walls. Darrel's chest tightened at the sound. He knew the truth then. Darrel would never love again. When he'd given his heart to Jayden, the man had kept it. Darrel didn't want it back. Someone else might hurt him. Jayden never would. They couldn't be together. Darrel wouldn't risk causing any further harm, but he could do this. He could make Jayden burn. Darrel loosened his jaw and set a pace he knew would drive Jayden insane. Jayden's hips left the floor as he writhed and openly fucked Darrel's mouth.

The sounds coming from Jayden had Darrel's dick leaking. He didn't care if he soaked the front of his underwear. This would never be about him. He'd been burning for Jayden's hot body for so long, he never expected relief anymore. Darrel didn't deserve pleasure. His fingers curled around the edge of Jayden's jeans and tugged, dragging the material lower. He sucked the man's balls and fingered his asshole. Jayden tried holding Darrel's head as he begged for release. Darrel wanted to give it to him. He equally never wanted to stop. Soon, Jayden would come down from this high and hate Darrel for touching him. This moment would end, and—no doubt—Jayden would never let this happen again. He'd probably never allow Darrel to be alone with him again either. Possibly, they'd never speak. Right now, in this moment, Jayden was his again. Darrel's heart didn't know how to give that up.

"Darrel."

The sound of his name on Jayden's lips in the perfect turned on tone nearly had Darrel coming in his jeans. He lost control. His motions quickened. Jayden's dick beat at the back of his throat. Darrel hollowed out his cheeks, sucking hard. Jayden cried out. Hot, salty cum filled Darrel's mouth. His eyes fell closed as he swallowed and kept sucking. Jayden gasped for air beneath him. Darrel couldn't stop licking. His heart wouldn't let him stop. Darrel's lips found Jayden's stomach. He kissed his way upward until he found Jayden's mouth again. Love choked him. Their kiss was sweet enough to bring tears to Darrel's eyes. It never stopped hitting him anew. He'd lost the world when he'd lost Jayden. This would be their last kiss. His heart cried out in denial, but his brain knew the truth. He had to let Jayden go. Jayden would never love him again without a hint of bitterness. That was on Darrel. He couldn't change the past, but he could leave this one last good memory of them with Jayden. Maybe it would give him peace.

"Stay," Darrel whispered against his lips. "I'll run and grab the right screwdriver and fix what I can." Darrel hoped Jayden understood. He'd fix what he could, even if it broke him.

CHAPTER 6

I<small>T WAS LIKE NOTHING HAPPENED.</small> J<small>AYDEN DIDN'T</small> know if Darrel jerked one out at home before coming back with the right tool for the shelf. Whatever happened, it was as if they'd never touched. Not only had Darrel not made another move on him, Jayden hadn't seen the man in the two weeks since. Even Richie hadn't said the man's name. Darrel simply disappeared. On the other end of the spectrum, Jayden couldn't stop thinking about Darrel. But it was obvious Darrel wanted nothing to do with him.

When Jayden had dated Wyatt, and they'd broken up, Jayden had done everything he could to win the man back. Things he was still ashamed of doing. He didn't want to be that guy again. Just for once, he wished someone would go that far for him. When Jayden loved someone, he did it with everything he had. He wanted the same in return. That was why he was currently sitting at the diner, a mess of nerves, while waiting for Bay to arrive. Jayden wasn't a drinker, but he wished now he'd agreed to meet the man somewhere that served alcohol.

"Wow. Are you driving again?"

Jayden's head jerked up in surprise at the sound of Darrel's voice. He'd been staring at the menu as if his life depended upon it while trying to calm his nerves. Now his discomfort doubled. "Um. No. Bryce dropped me off."

Darrel sat. "Why? Do you need a ride back home?"

Jayden blinked. "Um."

"Hello, again. Sorry. I don't recall your name."

Jayden's eyes fell closed as Bay appeared at Darrel's side. When his eyes reopened, Darrel was looking between them. Jayden practically heard the puzzle pieces snapping together.

"Oh. Sorry. It's Darrel," Darrel said, coming to his feet. "I was having lunch with my partner and his husband," he said, motioning toward where

Wyatt and Benny sat nearby. Jayden flashed them an uncomfortable smile while Darrel kept talking. "When I spotted Jayden sitting alone, I thought I'd say hi and invite him to sit with us. Sorry. I didn't realize he was waiting for someone."

Bay shook Darrel's hand. His friendly smile never wavered. "It's nice to see you. Do you want to join your friends?" Bay asked, switching his gaze Jayden's way. "I don't mind."

Jayden shook his head while trying to keep smiling. "That's okay. Darrel doesn't usually have much time on his lunch break. I'd hate to hold them up."

"Enjoy your lunch," Darrel said, walking away.

Jayden fought not to watch him go. His eyes burned to take in the sight of Darrel crossing the room. Instead, he kept his gaze locked on Bay as the man sat.

"Hey."

Bay's smile brightened at Jayden's greeting. Even to his ears, it sounded breathless. "Hey to you too," he said, settling into his seat. "I have to say, when I called yesterday, I fully expected to get shot down."

Jayden's smile felt realer by the second. "Yet you still called."

"Of course," Bay said, sounding confident. "If you don't ask, the answer is always no. Plus, what kind of fool would I be if I didn't use your number after you gave it to me? I don't give up easily."

"I'm glad you called." As Jayden said the words, he realized they were true. Darrel being there was unfortunate, and it hurt, but Darrel didn't want him. Bay wanted to be there.

Bay's gaze moved over Jayden's face. "No one looking at you now would know anything happened." A small smile touched Bay's lips. Jayden's breath caught. This was a different smile. Jayden knew immediately not many people saw this real side of Bay. "You're gorgeous."

Heat rushed to Jayden's cheeks. He'd never been good at taking compliments.

Bay chuckled. It was the sexy laugh Jayden remembered from when he couldn't see. "I'll change the subject since I can see you don't like compliments."

"Thanks for that," Jayden said, his embarrassment doubling. "It's not that I don't like compliments. I don't get them often."

"Bullshit."

A laugh escaped Jayden at Bay's open disbelief.

"I thought we were changing the subject. How have you been?"

"So we are." Bay carried the conversation, holding Jayden's attention throughout their meal. They had so much in common and knew a lot of the same people. The drive to help people was something that mattered quite a bit to them both. It gave them a lot to talk about. Before Jayden realized it, they'd eaten their food, moved on to dessert, and now finished coffee. He'd fully expected to know the exact moment Darrel left, but Jayden didn't notice. The waitress kept dropping hints they were holding one of her tables hostage. Jayden intended to tip her well.

Proving his thoughts mirrored Jayden's, Bay snagged the ticket before Jayden could get to it. "I guess we should let someone else have a chance to eat."

Jayden stood. "Yeah. I'm pretty sure our waitress thinks we've wasted her day."

"I plan to compensate her for allowing me to enjoy such a sexy man's company for as long as possible," Bay said with a wink.

To Jayden's surprise, this time, he didn't experience an ounce of embarrassment. "Same."

Without waiting to see Bay's reaction, Jayden pulled his wallet from his back pocket and tossed a few bills on the table. When his gaze shifted back Bay's way, he found the man still watching him, as if he'd been waiting to reclaim Jayden's attention.

"See me again."

Jayden took a breath, trying to squelch the hope rising in his chest. No one had looked at him in a long time the way Bay looked at him now. It took every ounce of his self-control to keep from sounding over enthusiastic. "All right."

Bay's mouth lifted in one corner in a sexy, self-satisfied way. "I know they haven't released you to drive yet. How are you getting home?"

"I'll take a cab," Jayden answered with a shrug.

"No," Bay said, heading for the register. "I'll take you home."

Behind Bay, Jayden pressed his lips together, trying to fight a smile that wouldn't abate. "Okay."

Bay paid the check before focusing on Jayden once more. "I like this agreeable version of you. What should we do now?"

Jayden held the door open for Bay. He eyed the man from head to foot, not bothering to hide the heat in his gaze as Bay passed. "I'm sure we'll think of something." Honestly, Jayden had no plan beyond possibly stealing a kiss, but he wanted Bay to know he was interested. It was past time he stopped pining for a life he'd never have and try for a life he could.

———

PETTING RICHIE and Bryce's dog Beau was the only thing keeping Darrel sane. He shouldn't have come here. Darrel couldn't stay away. Seeing Jayden on a date with someone else was the worst sort of hell. He couldn't even imagine how Jayden had felt catching him with someone else. Darrel had decided to let the man go. He really had. It wasn't happening. If anything, the past two weeks of not speaking to Jayden had deepened Darrel's obsession. He'd never love anyone else.

Richie held out a cup of coffee. "How much longer do you plan to pretend you're here to see me?"

Darrel looked up from where his fingers ran through Beau's white and gray fur. He shook his head at Richie's silent offer. "I'm not pretending," Darrel argued.

Richie snorted and took a sip of his coffee before setting Darrel's cup aside.

Darrel smiled at the sound. "I'm not," he repeated. "I thought you were smart enough to realize I came for Jayden."

"And if he doesn't come home tonight?" Richie asked, keeping his gaze locked on his cup and saving Darrel's pride.

Despite the pains in his chest, Darrel stiffened his spine. "Then I'll have to get over it, but it changes nothing. I still plan to throw myself on his mercy." Darrel glanced over, meeting Richie's gaze. "For real, I can't keep this up."

"Maybe it's high time you told him everyone leaves you, and he scared you shitless because you knew he was the one person you couldn't stand losing, so you destroyed him first." Bryce said the words in one quick burst as he joined them on the couch, as if he expected Darrel would run away the moment Bryce tried talking about it.

Darrel looked away and went back to petting Beau. "See. This is why nobody talks to you about anything. You're too fucking smart. No one likes being laid bare."

"Wah. Wah," Bryce said, making him smile. "I

know men don't talk things over. Do you want to take action? Then take action," Bryce said, popping back to his feet.

Darrel didn't immediately stand.

Bryce's eyebrows rose. "Well, come on."

Since Richie didn't look like he intended to help Darrel out, Darrel came to his feet. Bryce headed through the kitchen and Darrel followed. When Bryce held the back door open for him, Darrel wondered if Bryce was putting him out, until Bryce followed him outside. The porch light cast a glow on Bryce's face. Not for the first time, Darrel marveled over Bryce's perfection. Light green eyes and dark hair combined with flawless chiseled features made Bryce one of the most beautiful men on the planet. But to Darrel, there was no one who held a candle to Jayden.

Darrel eyed the pool as they passed. A few months earlier, Bryce had lived in a house equally as nice as this place, but Bryce had been fired from his position as a psychologist for the Central Crime Divisional—a combination of federal law enforcement agencies operating in one place. At first, Bryce and Richie had downsized to a smaller place. Then, it turned out the agents who'd been Bryce's patients hadn't appreciated being shuffled from a doctor they trusted. Every single one had chosen to continue seeing Bryce in private practice, forcing the Bureau to negotiate a private contract with Bryce. Now Bryce made twice the money, worked from home, and employed Richie for security and Jayden as a medical assistant.

When Darrel realized Bryce was headed for the guest house, he rushed to catch up. "What are you doing?"

Bryce pulled his keys from his pocket. "I'm letting you inside so you can wait for Jayden."

"I don't think he'll like that."

Darrel could practically hear Bryce's eyes roll. "While you're here, you can put that damn glass case together again. That's as good of an excuse as any to be here."

Darrel hesitated in the open doorway. Bryce gave him a little shove. "Go. You don't want to talk. You don't want to act. What the fuck do you plan then, Darrel? I know it's not waiting for Jayden to come crawling back to you. If so, fuck you. You don't deserve that."

"Ouch." Darrel meant it too. Ouch. He hadn't expected that from Bryce.

"Call me a liar," Bryce taunted.

Darrel shook head. "No. I deserved that. It should've come from Jayden, though."

"Well, tough shit," Bryce said, refusing to take mercy on him. "You have exactly two choices here. Either you choose Jayden—and I mean really fucking choose him, like a real man would—or you can leave him the fuck alone once and for all. No looking back."

"I can't walk away." Darrel didn't hesitate making the confession. He meant it.

Bryce motioned inside the house. "Then get to work fixing things, because Jayden is too nice to tell you to go to hell, and I'm not nice enough to coddle you while you only love him half ass." Bryce moved a step closer, and Darrel wondered for a second if Bryce would do him physical harm. "I love him too." Bryce meant it. No one could look at him and call him a liar. "Maybe it's not the same way you love him, but don't you for a second think I won't put all my skills into ensuring Jayden never lacks for a single fucking thing without you if you fuck this up. Then, once I have him straightened out, *I will end you*."

"Goddamn," Darrel said before he could stop it. "He's lucky to have you."

Bryce took a step back and shook his head,

looking sad. "No. I'm the lucky one. Just like you. The difference between us is, I realize it. Now fix this."

Darrel watched Bryce walk away. In that moment, he understood exactly why Bryce got paid the big bucks, and how right Jayden had been to stay the man's friend.

———

BAY'S HOUSE was freaking amazing. Jayden kept trying not to look at everything, but damn. He'd thought the new house Bryce and Richie had bought was great, but this place... wow.

He peered through the French doors, taking in the pool lighting up the darkness. Before he could gather his thoughts about the beautiful three-story home, Bay's hands slid across Jayden's hips, urging him back against his chest. Jayden's heart jumped into his throat. Bay smelled like the millions he was obviously worth. Jayden felt like a goddamn fool because he wasn't sure he wanted this. Then, Bay's lips lightly brushed Jayden's nape, and he wasn't so sure he didn't want it. He was so goddamn confused. His body responded despite his fucked-up brain. A ragged breath escaped him, and his cock stirred as Bay's mouth moved to Jayden's neck.

Bay gently turned Jayden in his arms. Their lips met. Jayden's heart sank. It was nice, but no passion exploded through their kiss. He wasn't giving up. Bay crowded his space, going flush against him, giving Jayden a solid feel of the man's erection. It was impressive. In fact, everything about Bay was amazing. Still, unconsciously, he took a step back, keeping an inch between them while not breaking their kiss.

While cupping Jayden's face, Bay leaned away. His gaze moved over Jayden's features, searching. He dropped his hands. "What's his name?"

Everything inside Jayden shattered. He was fucking this up, and Bay didn't deserve this. "It's not like that."

Bay smiled. It was self-deprecating, and Jayden hated himself. "If there's one thing I'm an expert at, it's kissing someone who's secretly in love with someone else. So, who is it?"

Fuck. Jayden tilted his head back and stared at the ceiling, wishing like hell he could lie and fake his way through this. He just needed a little time.

"It's okay," Bay said, bringing Jayden's gaze back his way. The man really did look fine. "You can talk to me. I wouldn't have asked if I didn't want to know."

Jayden shook his head. His throat hurt. "It doesn't matter. We've been over for a while now. It's just me. I haven't dated anyone else since, and I'm trying to move on. But I get that it's not fair to ask you to be patient with me."

Bay moved to the couch and sat. He gave the spot beside him a pat. "Actually, I'm a pretty patient guy, but not without knowing the story."

Giving in, Jayden crossed the room and joined Bay on the couch. They'd had a great day, talking and getting to know each other. After lunch, they'd ended up playing golf, which was something Jayden hadn't done in years, and wasn't very good at, especially since he couldn't see what he was doing. Bay hadn't laughed at him. Not once. In fact, he'd purposcly missed several shots, refusing to take the game seriously. Afterward, they'd gone to dinner and hogged another table for two hours before finally deciding to quit holding servers hostage and go back to Bay's place. Jayden didn't want to ruin his shot with Bay, but neither did he want to waste anyone's time.

"There's not a lot to tell, really. I fell in love. We moved in together and started talking about spending our lives together. Then, one day, I came home from work a little too early."

Bay groaned.

"Yep," Jayden said, realizing he had more to say than he first thought. "But really, the problem is me. I always fall in love with people, thinking they'll treat me the way I treat them."

"That's how it's supposed to work, but I'm the same."

Jayden felt a real spark of connection with Bay at the claim. The man meant it. He'd been there too. Jayden turned sideways and held Bay's stare. "I keep telling myself, I'm going to let this go. Move on and be with someone who wants to be with me. Someone who I can trust and..." A sad smile pulled at Jayden's lips. Even he wasn't sure where he was headed with this.

"Then you self-destruct," Bay finished for him, proving he understood.

"Why are you single?" Jayden asked with a laugh. "Really. Any fool would be lucky to have you, including me."

Bay pulled a face.

Jayden's heart sank.

"About that," Bay said, sounding guilty. "I think I should explain."

Jayden thought Bay should fucking explain too. He couldn't be the other man. The one who acted like it was nothing when Bay's man came home. He just couldn't. Jayden's heart couldn't take another fucking thing. He wasn't that guy. Jayden wouldn't do to someone else what had been done to him.

CHAPTER 7

HE SHOULD LEAVE. DARREL HAD FINISHED PUTTING the shelf together half an hour ago, but he couldn't make himself walk away. The whole place smelled like Jayden. No one would ever know how much he missed his house smelling just like this. He could still remember the exact day he'd come home, and the house no longer held a single hint of Jayden's cologne.

Keys jangled in the door. Darrel came to his feet. For some reason he couldn't explain, he didn't want to get caught sitting there on the couch—like he'd been waiting all day. Jayden stared down at his hands in confusion, as if trying to figure out why the door wasn't locked. His chin lifted. Their gazes met. Darrel shifted uncomfortably even as his heart rate kicked up.

"Bryce let me in," Darrel explained. "To put your shelf together again," he added, because even to him, Darrel sounded like a stalker.

Jayden's gaze moved to the glass shelving. "Oh," he said absently, sounding like his throat hurt. "Thank you. I'm sorry you had to do it again. When you put it together last time, I didn't think Bryce and Richie would close on this house quite so fast."

"It's not a problem." It really wasn't. Darrel would assemble the goddamn shelf a million times if it meant he'd get the chance to be alone with Jayden. He cleared his throat. "Listen, about earlier, I didn't mean to interfere in your date with the doctor. I just saw you sitting there alone, and—"

"It wasn't a date," Jayden said, interrupting him and causing an unwanted spurt of hope to rise in Darrel's chest. "Well, it was," Jayden tacked on, immediately killing it. "At first, it was," he added, confusing the hell out of Darrel. "Then, after lunch, we spent the rest of the day together, getting to know each other. Then we went back to his place, and it wasn't a date any longer."

"Okay," Darrel said, dragging out the word. "I'm confused."

"He's married," Jayden explained, enraging Darrel.

"What the fuck? He took you on a date and he's married? What kind of bastard does that? I mean, I guess I have no right to judge since I'm a bastard too. But still, what the fuck?"

Jayden's mouth lifted in one corner and he shook his head as if amused by Darrel's rant. He moved to the couch and sat. "They're split up—legally. He's already filed for divorce, so I guess, that's still not the reason it wasn't a date."

Darrel couldn't resist the urge to be near Jayden. He closed the distance between them and sat beside him. "I'm not following."

Jayden's hands lifted before falling back to his lap, but his gaze never wavered from Darrel. "He kissed me, and everything felt wrong. So we started talking it out. Bay was telling me the story of how he came home early from a conference and caught his husband cheating, and everything he said sounded exactly like you and me. He moved here to get away from his old life. Plus, his family lives here. Honestly, we have a million things in common. I'd planned to move to San Diego to get away from you."

Darrel's throat swelled. "You were trying to get

away from me?" The idea hurt more than Darrel expected.

While still holding his stare, Jayden nodded. "I've been cheated on before. That wasn't new, but losing you..." Jayden shook his head. "I couldn't keep running into you everywhere I went. When you had surgery on your shoulder and didn't tell me, I felt almost every bit as betrayed as having you cheat on me. How fucked up is that? You belong to me, Darrel. Even if you're not mine," he said almost too quietly to hear. Jayden looked away and stared at the wall. Darrel couldn't stop staring at him. "I couldn't even kiss the guy." Everything he said hit home with Darrel. He did belong to Jayden whether he did or not. Maybe that would've changed if Jayden had moved. Darrel had a gut feeling it would not.

"I would've come after you," Darrel said, surprising even himself with the confession. "If you'd moved," he clarified. "I would've shown up on your doorstep and dogged your every move. You've never known stalking like I would've hounded you if you'd left me behind." Jayden's gaze moved his way. There was hope in the man's eyes, and Darrel couldn't stop. "The same goes for you replacing me. You can. It would be so fucking easy for you to find someone else who's a billion times better than me, but there won't be a damn thing simple about it," Darrel promised. "Because I don't deserve you or your mercy, but I'm won't go away. You don't have to forgive me. In fact, you shouldn't, but I love you, Jayden. I can't give you up."

Darrel inched closer. Jayden's gaze dropped to Darrel's mouth. Before his chance passed, Darrel captured the man's lips. He felt Jayden's breath shudder. Then, Jayden's bottom lip was between his teeth. Darrel's heart was on the line. He swiped his tongue over Jayden's lip and the man licked him back. With Jayden's face held between his hands, Darrel deepened their kiss. As always, there was so much love and passion between them, Darrel marveled over how they didn't spontaneously combust. Darrel tried shifting closer, determined to taste all of Jayden. Jayden's hands flattened against his chest. With the slightest push, he held Darrel away. Pain radiated from the man's eyes. Darrel couldn't breathe.

"You're confusing me."

Darrel's heart was breaking inside his chest. "I'm sorry."

Jayden shook his head. "I don't want you to apologize. That means you regret me."

"Not possible." Darrel had never meant anything more.

"I'm not sure I want this. My heart hurts too much. The last time I kissed you, I didn't hear from you for two weeks afterward. The time before that, it was three weeks."

He didn't hesitate giving Jayden space. Darrel had known in his heart Jayden wouldn't take him back. While keeping his gaze averted, Darrel stood. "Yeah. I get that. I'm a fuck up." He motioned toward the door, hoping like hell he could make it without falling apart. "I'll get out of your life. You don't deserve this." Jayden said something behind him. Darrel couldn't hear a thing past the ringing in his ears. Every damn day, he lost a little more of himself. Today, Darrel feared he'd finally lost the final piece. Something fundamental to him continuing to live, broke. His feet didn't stop moving until the door closed between them. That was where he fell apart.

JAYDEN WAS helpless as Darrel scrambled to get away. He hadn't meant for Darrel to leave. Fuck. He didn't know what to do. Jayden didn't want

Darrel to go. He didn't know if he could take it if he stayed. They'd never discussed why Jayden hadn't held on to Darrel the first time around. Jayden needed that. He couldn't spend the rest of his life worrying he wasn't good enough or if Darrel was too weak-natured to hold down a real relationship. Either way, he couldn't let Darrel leave in this state and thinking Jayden was done.

Jayden opened his texts, intent on apologizing to Darrel. A mile-long unread text stared up at him beneath Darrel's name. He had no idea how he missed it before now. Jayden scrolled up and checked the date. It had been sent a few days before he'd been released from the hospital. The last day Darrel had come to see him. Jayden held his breath and read.

Darrel: *I've never been a good man. Not before you, during you, or after you left. When we met, you were dating Wyatt. I told myself you were better off with him. He's a great guy. And still, I went home after every time I saw you, wishing you were mine and dreaming you'd look at me just once the way you looked at him. Then, you were single, and I told myself to give you space. I lie a lot to myself, but the biggest lie I ever told was that I could let go of the fantasy of you. The crazy thing is—I never really daydreamed about the sex, which I do miss like crazy, but fuck if I'm touching* anyone else, because I belong to you. Every time I thought about having you, it was always kissing you. Holding you. Linking my fingers through yours and hanging on.

Then, one night, you turned up on my doorstep. You looked at me the way I always hoped you would. It happened without me having to do a thing. You found me on your own. I thought I'd won the damn lottery. Like most lottery winners, I threw it all away. Not because I didn't love you, but because I more than love you. You're an obsession. A crazed mind will take you down a million roads. Each one darker than the last. Every time someone flirted with you, and everyone flirts with you. Jesus. Men and women, it doesn't matter. Everyone takes one look at you, and they're in your pocket. My fucked-up brain had a field day with that. The more I fixated upon you, the tighter I held on. The harder I clung, the more everything unraveled inside my head. Every day, I became more and more certain you'd find someone better. Because, hell, everyone is better than me. What I did to you, it wasn't weakness. I wasn't tempted away. There's no one out there who can upstage you or touch my heart. It was crazed obsession, making me see problems that weren't there. I had to destroy myself, so I could rebuild myself better. Loving you, that hasn't changed. You're the one for me, even if we're never together again. I'm not saying, if you don't take me back, I'll never date again. Maybe I will someday, but my heart will always know *what it's missing. You're the strongest person I know. You'll be fine no matter what. You can get past these injuries, and you can survive me. But I haven't survived you. Not really. To be honest, I don't want to, because I need the world to see I kept my unspoken vow to love you until death do we part.*

Jayden's vision blurring had nothing to do with moving the phone too far away from his face. He blinked, fighting back the burning behind his eyes as his gaze moved over the words a second time. Jayden didn't give himself time to think. The moment he finished the last line of Darrel's text, Jayden tossed the phone aside and headed for the door. If he hurried, maybe he could catch Darrel. If not, maybe Bryce would help him find the man. Jayden shot out the door and ran into a solid wall of chest.

Darrel reached out to steady him. Tears streamed down the man's face. "I couldn't make myself leave."

"Good," Jayden said, closing the final inch between them and capturing the man's lips. He walked backward while holding on to Darrel's shirt, towing him inside while never breaking their kiss. "Don't go," Jayden begged as he dragged the man over the threshold.

Darrel kicked the door closed behind him. "I won't," he promised, deepening their kiss.

Jayden tugged at the man's shirt, needing their skin to touch. No one hurt him the way Darrel did, and no one loved him as much as Darrel did. Most all, Jayden had never loved anyone like he loved Darrel. He knew in his heart no one would ever take the man's place.

"Give me this," Jayden said, pushing Darrel's shirt up his chest.

In one quick motion, Darrel whipped the material over his head and tossed it aside before reclaiming Jayden's mouth. Jayden's breath caught as his palms collided with Darrel's hard chest. He'd missed touching this delicious body. Darrel was six feet and four inches of hard muscle and strength. He was naughty yet gentle, but he could be hard and controlling. Jayden's fingertips traced every cut line of Darrel's stomach before reaching for the button of his jeans. Nothing else mattered. He was tired of fighting. Jayden missed the passion. He'd never kissed anyone who made him feel like this. Not before Darrel or after him.

Jayden loosened the button on Darrel's jeans and slowly slid the zipper down. "Come to bed with me," Jayden cajoled against the man's lips.

Darrel didn't answer right away. Instead, he took his time, gently nipping at Jayden's lips. Jayden's stomach quivered with desire. "In a minute," Darrel finally said as he leaned away and eyed Jayden's body. His mouth lifted in one corner as he snagged the hem of Jayden's shirt. His gaze met Jayden's. Jayden's breath caught at the lust burning in Darrel's eyes. He dragged the material higher until Jayden lifted his arm, allowing Darrel to pull the shirt up and over his head. Darrel tossed it away. "Now, you can lead the way."

Jayden felt a blush creep up his face as he turned away and headed for the bedroom. Only Darrel had the power to make him feel so on display. He'd been shirtless countless times in his life. Darrel made him feel like it was a show just for him. Jayden fought the urge to glance over his shoulder as he led Darrel to his bed. He swore he could feel the man's stare stroking his skin. When he reached the edge of the bed, Darrel overcame him. His hot chest pressed against Jayden's back. The man's strong arms encircled Jayden's waist. His mouth opened over the side of Jayden's neck as his hands found the button of Jayden's jeans. Jayden's head fell back against Darrel's shoulder. His eyes slipped closed. Darrel's nimble fingers made quick work of Jayden's jeans. He palmed Jayden's erection, stroking even as he sucked at Jayden's pulse.

Jayden was lost to the moment. Every worry disappeared. There was nothing bad between them. He was with the greatest love of his life, being cared for like only Darrel would. Darrel pushed Jayden's jeans down his hips, taking his underwear down too. He pushed until Jayden kicked free of the material, standing nude in Darrel's arms. Darrel's lips found his nape. Jayden's chin hit his chest, giving the man access to any place he wanted to kiss.

"Tell me what you want," Darrel demanded. His lips brushed Jayden's skin with each word.

Jayden's breath came out in gasps. A drop of pre-cum rolled down his length. "I want your hand down your pants every time you think my name."

"That's already true."

"Then I want you on the bed. Suited and lubed up." Jayden didn't care about anything except having Darrel inside him. It had been so damn long. He'd been starving since they split.

For a moment, Darrel's hold tightened on Jayden. "Is everything still in the bedside table?"

Jayden nodded.

Darrel's fingers encircled Jayden's jaw, gently

cupping his face and tilting his head back to capture his mouth. Their tongues stroked. Jayden's hunger grew. With one final nip, Darrel moved away. Jayden watched as the man stripped before finding a condom and lube. He climbed on the bed, giving Jayden a show as he rolled the condom down his length and coated it with lube. The man was proud in his nudity. He had every right. Jayden hadn't moved from his spot at the edge of the mattress the entire time for fear his knees would give out. Darrel made him weak.

While stroking his cock, Darrel met and held his stare. Jayden's tongue shot out, moistening his parched lips. Then, one knee hit the mattress, followed by the other until Jayden straddled the man's body. Their gazes never wavered even as Jayden's lips brushed Darrel's chest. He kissed a path up the man's body until their mouths met. Time stopped. Sound disappeared. Nothing existed outside their kiss.

Darrel's dick probed at his ass. Jayden shamelessly moved against Darrel's body, fucking the man's abs. The sensation of his cock, rubbing the delicious ridges, made Jayden insane. A puddle of pre-cum soaked Darrel's stomach. Moans and whimpers filled the room. Jayden no longer knew who they belonged to. Love and lust stirred inside him, fucking with his head and torturing his body.

"This isn't just sex," Jayden warned.

Darrel sounded breathless when he responded, "It never is with us."

"If we do this, you belong to me."

"That's always been true anyhow," Darrel said, leaving no doubt he meant every word. Then, Darrel pushed his way inside. He went still beneath Jayden. Their kiss slowed. Jayden rocked backward, taking the man deeper. His teeth sank into the soft flesh of Darrel's bottom lip as the man's thick cock stretched him wide. Darrel held tight. His body jerked like Jayden had sucked him dry and the man hadn't come yet. Darrel made him feel powerful— like he turned Darrel on to the point he was a mess. It was the world's strongest aphrodisiac. Jayden rode Darrel's dick, taking his pleasure and pulling out every trick to ruin Darrel for all others.

Darrel reached between them and palmed Jayden's erection, letting Jayden know he was close. Darrel never came first. He always ensured Jayden was taken care of before he let himself go. The man's muscles were hard as a rock. His jaw flexed from grinding his teeth. Jayden couldn't look away. He wanted to see Darrel snap.

Darrel stroked. A groan rose in Jayden's throat. He couldn't resist the release Darrel offered. Pressure pounded at his crown. Darrel was inside him. His eyes burned. The sensation of having Darrel between his thighs combined with Darrel's sexy reaction to having Jayden on his dick and the grip on his cock to drive Jayden over the edge. An orgasm hit, stealing a cry from Jayden.

His lips sought Darrel's. "I love you," Jayden whispered against Darrel's mouth.

At his confession, Darrel cried out. His grip tightened on Jayden, squeezing the air from Jayden's lungs. Darrel's clenched muscles jerked as he came. He gripped Jayden's hair, holding him in place as he bit at Jayden's lips. Everything about Darrel's orgasm was sexy as fuck. No one matched Darrel's intensity. Being with Darrel was beautiful and freeing. Sweat and cum slickened the space between them as they fought to get closer to each other. Jayden expected guilt or regret to settle in. Neither emotion darkened his brain. This was the man he wanted. It didn't matter what people would think. The past hurt, but not as badly as being without Darrel. His bitterness had held them both prisoner for too long. If he couldn't forgive Darrel, Jayden couldn't claim he loved him. One didn't exist without the other, and he fucking loved Darrel with every fiber of his being. Without Darrel, Jayden was incomplete.

Jayden rolled to the side, and Darrel came with him. He stroked Jayden's hair away from his face. Neither of them looked away from the other—like they were incapable of breaking their fragile new connection.

Darrel traced Jayden's cheek with his fingertips, lightly stroking. "I love you so much. Please don't regret me."

The backs of Jayden's eyes burned at Darrel's plea. "I've never regretted you. Not once. Don't give me a reason to start."

"Never," Darrel said, leaning in and pressing a light kiss to the corner of Jayden's mouth.

"I love you too," Jayden whispered as Darrel kissed him again.

"Let me take care of you," Darrel said before giving Jayden another light kiss and rolling from the bed.

Jayden enjoyed the sight of Darrel, nude and crossing the room to the bathroom. Fuck. Darrel had an amazing body. Darrel moved around inside the bathroom. The sound of water running filled the silence before Darrel came back with a wet washcloth. Jayden barely blinked as Darrel cleaned the mess from his skin. Chill bumps rose every place the man touched. Darrel was always gentle with him, as if caring for something precious.

With the mess cleaned away, Darrel slid into bed beside Jayden. They didn't speak. Instead, they stared at each other, as if scared words would ruin the tenuous connection they'd formed. Darrel linked his fingers through Jayden's. The confessions he'd read in Darrel's text came roaring back, making Jayden smile.

"What?"

Jayden shook his head at Darrel's question. "Just happy," he said, incapable of expressing how much he'd needed every single word Darrel had typed. Darrel deserved the same honesty from Jayden. The realization left Jayden weak with fear. Until now, he hadn't told a soul. While staring into Darrel's eyes, Jayden knew he could trust Darrel not to think less of him for being scared shitless.

DARREL COULDN'T STOP GAZING at Jayden. At his lowest, when he'd been certain all hope was lost, Jayden had thrown open the door and saved him. It was funny how the man always did that. He came to Darrel right when Darrel hit the point of no return. Darrel's fingers skimmed Jayden's stomach. He couldn't stop touching him, ensuring Jayden was real. There was always a chance his mind had snapped, making him see things that weren't there.

"I won't get better." Jayden said the words quickly—like they'd burst from his chest and taking Darrel by surprise.

"What?" Darrel asked, going up on his elbow, ready to comfort Jayden in any way the man needed.

Jayden looked so worried, Darrel found himself petting the man, stroking his skin and trying to comfort him as Jayden explained. "That's what I found out at my last doctor's appointment. The one I had the last time you put my shelf together," he clarified, as if he expected Darrel wouldn't remember. "I won't get better than I am now. My days of driving, working as a paramedic, and a thousand other things are over. My eyes are as healed as they're going to get. You're the first person I've told." Jayden blinked, as if fighting back tears, but they didn't fall.

Darrel wanted to fix things. This was way out of his area of expertise. "I'm so sorry, baby." He knew how much helping people meant to Jayden. His words felt inadequate.

Jayden shrugged. "Sometimes, it hits at the worst times, and I can't believe this is the rest of my life. I mean, when you go to the doctor, you expect them to fix you. You're never prepared to be unfixable. Other times, I think maybe I was supposed to end up here. I've only been working with Bryce a few weeks, but I've met so many people who've been traumatized in similar ways. Maybe this is what I should've been doing all along, working with these people."

There was never a day that went by when Darrel wasn't a little more impressed by Jayden's innate goodness. His heart was bigger than anyone Darrel had ever met. "You're so goddamn strong. I'm proud to know you."

"I don't feel strong," Jayden whispered—like confessing a dirty secret. "For example, I wanted you to kiss me earlier, but when you did, I panicked. I don't know if I have what it takes to hang on to you."

"You're the only one who has what it takes," Darrel said without hesitation. Jayden was the first and the last to tie him down. "But I can already see, it'll take drastic measures to prove I'll only ever come home to you. Since you can't tolerate living at my place again, I'll find a new one. We can live there, and you can watch me come home every night until you're finally convinced you're the only one for me."

Jayden chewed his bottom lip for a moment before focusing on Darrel. "The last time you asked me to take you back, you accused me of rushing things. Now you're ready to move back in together —like nothing happened."

Darrel shook his head. He had more regrets than ten men put together. "I shouldn't have said that about rushing things. It's not true. That's not why—"

"I know," Jayden said, interrupting Darrel as if he couldn't take hearing the words. "I got your text."

Fuck. He'd forgotten to erase it from Jayden's phone. When he'd seen Jayden with his eyes uncovered, everything had crashed in on him. He'd known then, Jayden didn't need him any longer. The knowledge had crushed him to the point he couldn't think of anything else. Darrel had rushed from the hospital and hadn't thought about that text since.

Before Darrel could think of something to say,

Jayden floored him. "You could live here." Uncertainty laced each word Jayden said. The more he spoke, the firmer his voice became. "This place is part of my incentive package. At first, I thought Bryce was just saying that to make me feel better about living here. Now that I've been at it for a few weeks, I realize he's given me a real job. He's had a temp person until now. I didn't know how important this position was for everyone involved."

As much as Darrel wanted to revisit the topic of living together, the excitement in Jayden's voice had him needing to know more. "What exactly are you doing for Bryce?"

"There's not a huge difference between this and my old job, in truth. I evaluate the patients when they come in, taking their vitals and making sure Bryce has an updated list of their medications. If someone has a panic attack during a session, I'm there to recheck their vitals and make sure they're not having a heart attack. Sometimes, people have to be transferred to a hospital." Jayden's smile grew as he talked. "Everyone Bryce sees has been through something traumatic, so they ask me about my scars. Once they hear my story, they relax. I belong here."

There was no way Darrel would ask Jayden to

move after that speech. Whether Jayden realized it or not, he was looking at the bright side of his problems, making the best from the worst. Jayden's attitude was one of the biggest reasons Darrel had such a hard time letting go. The man was filled with hope. It was impossible to hear him speak and not have optimism about the future. His future was with Jayden.

"Every time we talk, you make a thousand wishes appear in my head."

A line appeared between Jayden's brows. It cleared away as quickly as it appeared. A bright smile lit his face. "That's an odd thing to say, but— for some reason—it still felt like a compliment."

"That's because it was," Darrel said, settling down on his side and pillowing his head with his arm.

Jayden rolled, holding Darrel's stare. "I've missed you," he whispered, as if admitting a dirty secret.

There was nothing Darrel wouldn't do to keep hearing things like that from Jayden even if it meant moving at a snail's pace until they were healed. "Tell me what you need to make everything right between us," Darrel said before he could change his mind. "If you say, let's take things one day at a time, we will. If you need to know exactly where I am every second, and have me come home to you every night, I can do that. You're the one in charge of this, okay? I just want to be with you. You're the love of my life. I'll take as much or as little of you as you're willing to give."

Jayden's gaze moved over Darrel's face, searching. His expression gave no hint to his thoughts. A slow smile spread across his face. "Do you have any vacation days left after spending all that time in the hospital with me?"

Whatever Jayden had in mind, Darrel was in. "I didn't use any of my time. The first two days were mandatory leave after the explosion. After that, I switched shifts with someone on third. I've still got almost two weeks left for the year. Why?"

Jayden didn't answer. His smile grew before he inched closer and kissed the corner of Darrel's mouth. As their lips brushed, Darrel's curiosity muted. Whatever Jayden had planned could wait a few hours. Nothing mattered as much as the man's kiss. With a tug and a roll, he had Jayden pinned beneath him. Their tongues met and stroked. Darrel could barely breathe around the love choking him. He couldn't lie to himself, he wanted to rush Jayden. Every second he'd spent away from this man who was his whole damn world was a moment he needed back. Until he had Jayden locked down, Darrel knew he'd never breathe another easy breath.

Jayden's mouth moved to Darrel's jaw. Darrel tightened his hold on the sheet on either side of Jayden's head, trying to cling to reality. Tiny kisses trailed down his jaw to his neck before Jayden kissed a path to his ear. A shuddered breath left Darrel as Jayden's teeth sank into his lobe. "Let's go back to the beach. To the same spot where everything was perfect. Just for a few days. Just you and me." Darrel had no clue how Jayden sounded so level headed when he couldn't capture a single lucid thought. "We can figure out everything else when we get back. For now, let's just spend a few days reveling in having us back. I want you all to myself."

That final bit was all Jayden had to say. Darrel didn't need convincing. All Darrel required for survival was Jayden. "I'm in."

I'M IN. Funny how those two words stole Jayden's heart, leaving him breathless. Soon, they'd be secluded from the world. Jayden needed that more than air right now. Darrel's lips skimmed Jayden's chin before moving down his neck. Jayden knew the man had kissed the path of his scar from the explosion. His heart skipped a beat. He'd been so busy, wrapped up in his problems, Jayden hadn't truly considered how Darrel must've felt. They'd proven being apart didn't dampen their love. If Darrel had been the one hurt, Jayden would've come unglued.

Jayden massaged every place on Darrel he could reach, silently trying to comfort the man. Darrel moved lower. His teeth scraped Jayden's nipple. Thoughts of comfort disappeared. He'd forgotten how oral Darrel was. The man loved using his tongue and mouth to toy with Jayden. Jayden had purposely blocked the memory, hoping he could find someone else one day without being disappointed in everything about them. Darrel's tongue circled Jayden's navel before finding his hip bone. Jayden's entire body twitched in anticipation. He held Darrel's head and his breath.

Darrel palmed his cock. His lips brushed Jayden's crown in the lightest touch. Jayden's body jerked again. It was out of his control. His body was one giant nerve. Darrel was in charge. Jayden lost himself in Darrel's overwhelming passion. He writhed beneath the man's ministrations. With no idea how it happened, Jayden ended up with his cock down Darrel's throat and his knees spread wide, riding Darrel's lubed fingers while crying the man's name. In that moment, Darrel could've demanded anything. Not that he needed to. Jayden already intended to give the world to Darrel while expecting the same in return. It was well past time they went all in for each other.

CHAPTER 8

"You never really talk about it. How much can you see?"

Jayden eyed Darrel from his spot on the bed. "I can see your outline. You're wearing a white towel around your waist, but everything is a blur. I can't make out specific details." The white around Darrel's middle disappeared. A chuckle escaped Jayden. "And now you're nude."

"Is that an issue?"

Even to Jayden, his smile felt wicked. "Only if you stay way over there."

"Come join me, then you can see me with your hands."

Even though Jayden couldn't make out Darrel's expression, he could hear the smirk in the man's voice. "Was this whole conversation a ploy to get me to shower with you?"

"Maybe," Darrel said, dragging out the word.

Jayden climbed from the bed. He moved slow, dragging out the anticipation. They'd spent the past four days at the beach, staying in a private bungalow where no one would disturb them. It was almost time to go home. Jayden wasn't ready to share Darrel again. Four days felt like nowhere near enough time to make up for the months they'd been apart.

The closer he got to Darrel, the clearer the man's features became. Darrel chewed his bottom lip. His gaze ate Jayden alive. He'd never seen a man look hungrier. His cock stood proud, waiting for Jayden's attention. Jayden quickly stroked the man's erection before squeezing past him and heading for the shower. A soft whimper escaped Darrel as he padded behind him.

Steam already filled the room from where the water waited for Darrel. Jayden felt Darrel's stare on his skin as he stripped. He intentionally took his time, ensuring Darrel got his show. The moment he was nude, Darrel overcame him and shuffled him inside the shower. Their mouths collided as the rain shower poured hot water down their bodies.

Darrel held Jayden's face between his hands, controlling their kiss. The move left him open for Jayden to play with the man's body. He gently ran his thumb ring over Darrel's crown, toying with the man's slit. A moan vibrated around their entwined tongues. Darrel made Jayden simultaneously weak and strong. That one tiny moan owned Jayden. He needed Darrel to give him more. Jayden's back hit the cool shower wall. He couldn't look away from Darrel's hard expression as the man soaped their bodies. Darrel looked like he might snap at any moment. As much as Jayden wanted to see it happen, he equally craved whatever Darrel had planned for him. Darrel was patient and skilled. He had stamina that left Jayden begging for relief.

Darrel's sexy brown gaze held his. "You should see your face," Darrel said, sounding hoarse, and proving exactly how turned on he was. "You look so trusting—like you know I can and will make you fly."

"I'm high with love," Jayden admitted. He sucked in a breath as Darrel soaped his cock.

Darrel shuffled closer, palming both their erections. Their gazes never wavered. Before this trip, Jayden had feared they wouldn't be the same. He'd worried there'd be a part of him that believed

Darrel couldn't be trusted, or he didn't own all of this man. The opposite was true. They felt stronger than ever, as if everything bad had forged them like steel, making them unbreakable. Jayden swore he loved Darrel twice as much, and he'd never thought it possible to love him more.

"You make my soul sing," Darrel said, leaving Jayden torn between what the man did to his body and how Darrel fucked with his head. "Before you, I'm not sure I believed in anything."

Jayden held on to Darrel's shoulders as if his life depended on it. His knees were jelly. He had no idea how Darrel managed to keep talking so unaffected. Jayden breathed through the pleasure, getting hotter by the second. Still, he wanted Darrel's words. They kept him high. "And now?"

"I believe in everything, because I've seen heaven with you."

Jesus. Jayden didn't know how he was supposed to hang on to his sanity with Darrel saying shit like that while slowly pumping his cock. It wasn't fair. He had no control. Jayden locked his knees, trying to stay upright. Pleasure curled his toes. Pressure tightened his balls. His muscles tensed in anticipation.

Darrel pumped faster. His breaths quickened.

The sounds inside the shower added to Jayden's heightened lust. He openly fucked Darrel's palm, reveling in the sensation of his cock brushing Darrel's. Darrel's intensity doubled. Jayden couldn't look away. The man was so goddamn gorgeous, and he belonged to Jayden—forever.

An orgasm slammed into Jayden, stealing his breath. Before the final wave of pleasure washed over him, Darrel cried out. Their cum mixed between them, coating their skin. Darrel moved closer, pressing into Jayden and holding him against his chest. Jayden listened to the man's heart race. It thumped like Darrel had run a marathon. Jayden couldn't stop kissing the place where Darrel's heart slammed against his chest. That organ belonged to him.

"I love you," Darrel breathed, kissing his hair.

Jayden's eyes fell closed. The power of those words never lessened. "I love you too."

Darrel's lips skimmed the shell of his ear. "Are you ready to go home and face the music?"

Jayden hummed against Darrel's shoulder. "I'm not sure."

Darrel ran his fingers through Jayden's hair, making his eyes fall closed from the sensation. He loved when Darrel played with his hair. "How do you think Bryce will take the news?"

A groan escaped Jayden. He already knew it would be bad. "Not good. Not good at all."

"He loves you, so he'll forgive you."

Jayden ran his hands down Darrel's body, savoring the way the man felt against his palms. "Maybe. We'll find out tomorrow."

"Will you throw me over if Bryce doesn't approve?"

Jayden's hold automatically tightened on Darrel. Just the idea of being without this man again shattered his heart. "Never." Even Jayden heard the ferocity in his voice. Once his heart rate slowed, his thoughts cleared. "But Bryce loves me; he'd never expect that of me."

"Damn," Darrel said with a chuckle as he soaped their skin once more, cleaning their new mess. "I love hearing that possessiveness in your voice. As much as I'd like to think I'll give up being a jealous ass, I doubt it. It's good to know I'm not alone in my intensity."

A soft laugh escaped Jayden as he helped wash Darrel's body. "Be as jealous as you like, as long as you don't expect me to stop loving on Bryce."

Darrel snorted. "I'm not stupid enough to

expect that. Plus, the two of you are adorable together. It makes me smile to see you with him."

The more Darrel spoke, the larger Jayden's smile grew. "I'm so in love with you," he said, incapable of stopping himself. "You'll get sick of me saying that soon."

Darrel shook his head as he squirted some shampoo in his hand. "If you never say anything else but that, I'll die a happy man. Turn around."

Jayden bit back a smile and did as told. Darrel gently washed his hair. Jayden's body stirred to life like Darrel hadn't just blown his mind. With his eyes closed, he took in every sensation. Part of Jayden wished they were independently wealthy and could stay there forever. He'd miss Bryce too much. Tomorrow, they'd go home, and everything would change. For the better, he hoped. They still had tonight. One more night alone, away from the world, and completely focused on each other. Jayden reached over his head and cupped the back of Darrel's neck, towing him closer. When Darrel's body molded against his, a sigh escaped Jayden. Sometimes, Darrel had some of the corniest lines, but what the man had said earlier truly resonated with Jayden. Before Darrel, Jayden hadn't believed in much either. But this man, he'd dragged Jayden through hell and showed him heaven. Most of all, he'd proven soul mates existed. Darrel was his other half. No matter what happened, that would always be true.

DARREL DIDN'T KNOW how he made it back to Phoenix in one piece. He couldn't stop his eyes from drifting from the road to Jayden in the passenger seat. He'd never felt more blessed. This gorgeous, amazing man was his again. Had forgiven him. Would always be his. He wanted to tell the world. Darrel equally wanted to keep Jayden locked away and all to himself until the end of time. But Bryce was waiting, and Jayden needed his best friend too. Plus, at least one of them would need to work or they'd starve.

Watching Jayden smile while Bryce hugged him and spoke quietly against the man's ear made Darrel glad he'd found the strength to come back to Phoenix. Jayden needed the extra affection. Richie slapped Darrel across the back as he'd come through the door. That was as loving as their friendship got. Jayden wasn't like that. He was both feet in on every relationship in his life. Since the explosion, Darrel had come to realize Bryce was the same.

"Well, Richie. Now's your chance," Jayden said, laughter lacing each word. The happiness in Jayden's voice had Darrel massaging the ache in his chest. He'd never thought to see Jayden like this again. Darrel lived to see his man smile.

"For?" Richie asked, dragging out the word.

"I told you if I ever had a husband, I'd let you kiss him. Now, I know Darrel has been your friend for years."

"Wait. You're married?" Bryce said, interrupting.

Jayden didn't slow. "And you could've been kissing the man all you like before now."

"Seriously," Bryce said, trying to cut in again. "Did you get married?"

Jayden tried talking while laughing at Bryce's open shock. "But I did tell you I'd let you kiss my husband. Since that's Darrel, now's your shot."

"You fucking got married without me," Bryce yelled, losing his composure for the first time in Darrel's memory.

"Quick. Lie," Richie said, looking panicked.

Because it was Jayden, he didn't take Richie's obvious good advice. "I did," he said, reaching for

Bryce's hands. "But," he said loudly before Bryce could melt down, "it was a formality because we wanted to be married before living together again."

"Oh my god," Bryce breathed, sounding four steps beyond upset. "Not only did you get married without me, but you're moving too."

Jayden kissed him, silencing Bryce. Darrel searched his heart. Not an ounce of jealousy reared its head. They were friends, and they loved each other. Every kiss Jayden and Bryce shared was affection and nothing more.

Richie cast Darrel an amused glance. "I leave, and nothing. Not a single ruffled feather. Jayden marries you without telling him—crazy switch completely flipped."

Darrel shook his head. He was every bit as surprised to see this side of Bryce as Richie. Luckily, Jayden had things in hand.

"I'm not moving. Darrel plans to live here with me."

Richie chuckled. "One big, happy family. By the way, I'm not interested in kissing you."

Darrel tossed the man a wink. He loved Richie, but no one kissed him except Jayden.

Jayden and Bryce ignored them. "We are married, but we still want a wedding. We also sort of hoped, since the two of you didn't have a real wedding either…" Jayden paused and took a breath, as if he didn't like the way he came across. "I mean, Richie threw you a surprise wedding at the courthouse, and that was sweet. Darrel and I did a thing on the beach, which was awesome, but none of us had the huge wedding people talk about. Anyhow, we hoped—maybe—you might be interested in doing a huge double wedding." Jayden winced as the final word left his lips as if he expected Richie and Bryce to hate the idea. Darrel didn't give two shits. Jayden had already married him. He'd already won the world. If Jayden wanted to throw a huge thing, Darrel would go along with whatever, as long as it made Jayden smile. He had his dream husband already either way.

Bryce looked to Richie, his expression hopeful. A bright smile stretched Darrel's lips as Richie gently pushed Jayden out of the way and tugged Bryce into his arms. "You want this, don't you?"

Bryce chewed his bottom lip while eyeing Richie. Darrel tugged Jayden against his side. They were getting their wedding. It was in Bryce's gaze. He wanted to do the big wedding thing. Not only that, but the man obviously wanted to share that day with Jayden.

A soft chuckle escaped Richie. "I see it in your eyes. We're having another wedding. Lucky for you, I'd marry you a thousand times if you'd let me."

Darrel understood that sentiment. Jayden was brilliant. He knew exactly how to make everyone happy, especially Darrel. Jayden wrapped his arms around Darrel, going flush against him, and making everyone else disappear for Darrel.

"We should go home and let them discuss things."

Darrel couldn't stop massaging every place on Jayden he could reach. Home. His home was now with Jayden. Darrel couldn't fucking believe it. He didn't deserve this life, but he would. As long as he lived, Darrel would make sure Jayden was the happiest husband on the planet. As long as Darrel lived, he would cherish Jayden.

Charity Parkerson is an award winning and multi-published author with several companies. Born with no filter from her brain to her mouth, she decided to take this odd quirk and insert it in her characters.

*Seven-time Readers' Favorite Award Winner
    *2015 Passionate Plume Award Finalist
    *2013 Reviewers' Choice Award Winner
    *2012 ARRA Finalist for Favorite Paranormal Romance
    *Five-time winner of The Mistress of the Darkpath

Connect with her online:

--Join my street team: facebook.com/TeamCharityParkerson
    --Sign up for my newsletter: http://bit.ly/CharityNews

--Website: charityparkerson.com

--Facebook:
facebook.com/authorCharityParkerson

facebook.com/TheMenofSin

--Twitter: twitter.com/CharityParkerso